P9-DMR-426

Do you believe in magic?

"Do you know what you've done?"

Cam stood as tall as he could on trembling legs, straightened his tunic, and faced his master.

"I'm truly sorry," he said, and he was, for he'd hoped to travel with Quinn to outer earth. "Can you bring her back now?"

"Bring her back?" Melikar continued his distraught pacing. "I can't bring her back until she *chooses* to come back." He stopped to give his apprentice a red-eyed glare. "The difficulty is, she doesn't know this...."

Other Point Fantasy titles
you will enjoy:

Shadow of the Red Moon
by Walter Dean Myers

Princess Nevermore

DIAN CURTIS REGAN

SCHOLASTIC INC.
New York Toronto London Auckland Sydney

*For Jodi Koumalats and Dee Pace,
who've always believed in
magic and Mandrian truths*

If you purchased this book without a cover, you should be aware that this book is stolen property. It was reported as "unsold and destroyed" to the publisher, and neither the author nor the publisher has received any payment for this "stripped book."

No part of this publication may be reproduced in whole or in part, or stored in a retrieval system, or transmitted in any form or by any means, electronic, mechanical, photocopying, recording, or otherwise, without written permission of the publisher. For information regarding permission, write to Scholastic Inc., 555 Broadway, New York, NY 10012.

ISBN 0-590-45759-4

Copyright © 1995 by Dian Curtis Regan.
All rights reserved. Published by Scholastic Inc. SCHOLASTIC, POINT, and associated logos are trademarks and/or registered trademarks of Scholastic Inc.

12 11 10 9 8 7 6 5 4 3   8 9/9 0 1 2/0

Contents

Contents

1

The Wishing Pool

Princess Quinn raised both arms to steady herself as she balanced upon the wizard's footstool.

Tilting her head, she strained to hear the soft wish drifting down from the wishing pool high above.

"Come off that stool before you tumble over," grumbled old Melikar.

The wishing words were coming now. Another moment and —

"Princess!"

The force of the wizard's shout knocked Quinn off the footstool and onto the cobblestone floor. She landed in a heap of petticoats, buffeting her fall.

When Melikar turned away, she wrinkled her royal nose at him.

Then, remembering Melikar *was* a wizard, and probably *knew* when a person was being disrespectful behind his back, she pretended to be struck by an urgent itch, giving her nose a vigorous rub.

Quinn loved Melikar dearly, but his awesome power commanded her greatest respect. If anyone else had insisted she hop off the footstool, she'd have ignored them, and caught the wafting wish before it melted into the dank air of the underground chamber.

But she'd promised her mother, Queen Leah, she'd "obey Melikar as long as you insist on spending so much time with that old enchanter."

Besides, visiting the wizard's chamber was the *only* interesting part of her life nowadays.

Righting the footstool, Quinn squinted up through the blue-green pool. Long ago, Melikar cast a spell to keep the water from splashing into his chamber, *and* to keep the pool still and calm, creating a window to the other world.

Not only could wishes be heard, but sometimes outer-earth folk tossed coins into the pool to seal a wish. The coins would lie scattered across the chamber floor until Cam, the wizard's apprentice, swept them away.

"I don't know what fascinates you and Cam about those who live in the other world." Melikar thrust a candlewick into the fire and waited till it burst into flame. "They're an unhappy lot, coming to the pool all hours, wanting this and wanting that. Some wish with such intensity they wake me in the middle of the night. I've half a mind to cover the underside of the pool."

"Oh, Melikar, *no.*" Quinn grabbed the apricot sleeve of the wizard's robe, almost knocking the candle from his grasp. "This is the only place in the entire kingdom of Mandria where I can view the other world — it's a Mandrian truth," she added quickly so the wizard couldn't argue.

Mandrian truths could *not* be argued.

The look he gave her made her suspect he *had* seen the disrespectful wrinkling of her nose.

Melikar secured the candle in a spiked holder and moved to his workbench.

Gathering the full skirts of her sapphire gown, Quinn perched on the footstool, pulling her lion-colored braid to one side so she wouldn't sit on it. Her hair had been growing for all of her fifteen years.

"If it wasn't for the wishing pool," she said, continuing her argument, "I'd never know what the sky looks like, or trees, or stars."

The wizard finished sprinkling rue, wild yam, and pure gold dust into a flask — a concoction to soothe the king's stiff muscles. Lifting his head, he fixed Quinn's gaze with his translucent red eyes, as if her niggling worries didn't warrant any answers.

The princess blinked at him, like she used to do when she was young, trying to master the art of winking. "Please don't cover the pool."

He answered by popping a cork atop the flask. "I tend to forget those above don't have magic to change things. But a perfectly acceptable maiden wishing for beauty when wars abound up there seems as trifling as a Marnie wishing for rest."

Quinn smiled at his analogy. The Marnies, small creatures covered with soft fur from head to hoof, the same color as the gold they mined, never rested. Their sole purpose, their lifeblood, was helping others. In their bustling village, they made candles and furniture, tended Mandrian food-growing chambers, and supplied the kingdom with all its needs.

Quinn busied herself, touring Melikar's chamber, relishing sensations tingling through her from the aura of magic, which swirled within the chamber like mists rising from the underground bogs.

What made this place most inviting were flavors in the air. Quinn inhaled deeply, taking in the earthy aromas of spells and magic.

Shadows flickered mysteriously against cavelike walls. Furnishings were simple: a straw mattress for the wizard, a cot for his apprentice, and ornately carved oak furniture, made by Marnies.

She stopped by the hearth. Sometimes Melikar gazed into the fire for long moments, then told her and Cam stories of wars and other sadnesses.

But it wasn't all sad. He also told of parades, picnics, grassy meadows filled with galloping horses, and of great balloons rising into the air and floating away, carrying baskets full of outer-earth folk.

Her desire to see the other world grew more intense each day that brought her closer to her sixteenth birthday.

Sixteen.

The age a maiden stopped being a child and became a woman.

It was a Mandrian truth.

Closing her eyes, Quinn imagined a line of faceless suitors coming to court her until she chose one to marry — or the king chose one for her.

After that, her life would be a series of *have-to-dos;* her days full of royal protocol and childbearing. No more visits with the wizard, no more tarrying about the kingdom with Cam or Ameka, her royal tutor.

Her life would be a book already set forth.

"Here." Melikar's gravelly voice jolted her from daydreaming about her predictable future. "The potion for your father is ready. One advantage of those in the other world is not suffering stiff muscles from living under the damp ground."

Quinn wasn't ready to leave. The wishing pool bustled with activity today. As she watched, a young couple stepped upon the curved footbridge, stopping in the middle to embrace.

Quinn's heart twinged, longing to know what it was like to be touched the way the lad was touching the maiden.

She'd never been hugged; she was a princess. Even her parents were too formal to display affection.

"Quit dawdling."

Sighing, she reached for the flask. As her fingers curved around the warm glass, a great whirring noise and a flash of bright light knocked her once more to the cold, rock floor.

The flashy commotion was the materialization of Cam.

"Bats!" he exclaimed, looking bewildered. He peered at his surroundings, then at the magic ring he'd been trying to create with his limited enchanter's ability. "The ring was supposed to take me to the Marnies' candle chamber, not here. I twisted it three times and pictured exactly where I wanted to go."

"Cam of Mandria," the princess grumbled, wrestling to right her skirts and herself. She paused to smooth a bit of torn lace on her gown. "That ring never does the right thing at the right time."

"Candles were clearly *not* the object of your thoughts," muttered Melikar, glancing from his apprentice to the disarrayed princess.

Cam looked so forlorn, Quinn wished she hadn't spoken harshly. He'd worked diligently on the ring after she'd teased him about his magical failures. Softening her voice, she added, "What do I tell Mother? You've ruined my gown. You — "

"Devil dust!"

The wizard's outburst stopped Quinn. He was obviously annoyed by the noisy disruption of his work.

"Recast the spell, lad, and look it up in the *Book* to make sure you get it right this time. It needn't take three twists to make the magic work."

"Why couldn't you appear on the *other* side of the chamber?" Quinn asked, lowering her voice to appease Melikar. "Or simply *walk* through the portal like a *normal* Mandrian?"

When Cam didn't respond, she stopped dusting her gown to see why.

The look on his face told her he wasn't listening.

Then Melikar's words sunk in. The wizard had given his apprentice permission to open the *Mandrian Book of Magic*. Cam had never been allowed to touch it.

All the magic known to enchanters was in the _Book_. If the apprentice hadn't caused such a disturbance, Quinn was sure Melikar would have looked up the spell himself.

Cam caught her eye.

The two had discussed at great length traveling to the outer world together, but Cam didn't know the spell.

Quinn knew his thoughts matched hers. Now that the _Book_ lay open before him, it would be quite simple to find it.

His hand trembled as he turned the pages.

"Sire," Quinn began, knowing she must distract the wizard long enough for Cam to locate the spell. "Has any Mandrian ever traveled to the other world?"

Melikar studied her over the candle's flame. "Why?"

"Well, _someone_ needs to tell these folk who plead with us for wishes, we can't possibly grant them."

She kept one eye on Cam, whose lanky form curved over the _Book_. Dark hair covered his closed eyes as he mumbled magic words to the ring.

Melikar's eyes glistened blood-red in the flickering light. "They're not asking us to fulfill their wishes. They don't know we're here."

"Well, then, someone needs to tell them not to depend upon the wishing pool for answers." Quinn twisted her braid through her fingers, feeling pleased with her response.

A smile twitched the enchanter's mustache as he pinched a dash of turmeric into a flask, then scribbled a few notes on a scroll. "And I suppose you think you're best fit to bear this message to the other world?"

Behind the wizard, Cam moved to the huge cauldron bubbling upon the hearth. Picking up a ladle, he began to stir the thick liquid.

Quinn ignored Melikar's question, wondering why Cam had abandoned the *Book*. "Cam could go with me," she said, poking her finger into a dish of mixed herbs. "And if you send — "

"Princess," interrupted the wizard. "For no reason can you leave Mandria. Whether or not I can send you is another matter. Folk in the other world are different. If they discovered where you came from, they'd descend on us with shovels and dig up our rooftops."

"Oh, I'd never tell, and Cam — "

"Enough!" spoke Melikar, raising a robed arm. The chamber walls trembled as they did during outer-earth thunderstorms.

Quinn flinched, frightened by his response. It was a Mandrian truth not to question an elder's words, but sometimes she had to be reminded.

Melikar pointed a bony finger at her. "There's no magic in the other world. Centuries ago, all magical creatures were driven to the underground kingdoms. Cam would not endure long there."

Though absorbed by the wizard's tale, Quinn's eyes were drawn to the wishing pool. The water was swirling in a wide circle.

She caught her breath. Never before had she seen the water move.

Melikar, hunched over his workbench, did not notice the oddity. "It takes magic in one's surroundings to make the magic inside work. Cam would weaken as his magic faded. If he didn't return to Mandria within a short time, he would die."

The princess glanced at Cam. He wasn't listening to the wizard's warning. Later she'd tell him of this danger, making sure their journey lasted but a day.

"That," Melikar was saying, "is why our kingdom abounds with enchanted creatures." He leaned toward her, eyes wide, and whispered, "The middle of the earth holds magic."

A sudden knock at the portal drew Melikar away from his workbench.

Quinn was grateful for the messenger — who was

further distracting the wizard. Her own attention remained fixed upon the pool. She moved toward it, drawn, as if under a spell.

The faster Cam stirred the liquid in the cauldron, the faster the water swirled.

Taking a deep breath, the princess stepped into the circle of light beneath the pool. At the same instant, Cam began to whisper-chant:

> *"Anger, fear, love, and mirth.*
> *Send Quinn and Cam to outer earth."*

2
A Forbidden Spell

Hearing a scream, Cam stopped his stirring and chanting.

Quinn was rising toward the wishing pool!

Dropping the ladle, he raced to join her, tripped over the footstool, and smashed into the princess.

Before he could grab hold of her, she rose up through the pool and disappeared.

Cam sprawled on the cobbled floor, gaping at the turbulent water. The princess was gone — yet he was still here!

"Get up!" shouted Melikar, pacing beneath the pool, robes flapping with each angry step.

If the trembling walls of the chamber hinted at thunder before, they now shook with the force of an earthquake under the wizard's wrath.

Afraid to meet Melikar's eyes, Cam reached for the

magic ring with frantic plans of making a fast disappearance.

On second thought, staying to take the blame was more honorable — which was just as well since he'd dropped the ring when he collided with Quinn. He'd find it later.

Melikar helped him to his feet with a quick yank. "Do you know what you've done?"

Cam stood as tall as he could on trembling legs, straightened his tunic, and faced his master. "I'm truly sorry," he said. And he was, for he'd hoped to travel with Quinn to outer earth. "Can you bring her back now?"

"Bring her back?" Melikar continued his distraught pacing. "I can't bring her back until she *chooses* to return." He stopped to give his apprentice a red-eyed glare. "The difficulty is, she doesn't know this."

Cam took the whole burden upon his heart. "What have I done?" He trudged in a circle, mumbling to himself about the ring, the spell, and the question of why he hadn't gone with Quinn after he'd chanted both their names.

Quinn.

Alone in the other world. Without him to protect her.

Fear for the princess's safety, as well as fear for his

very life when the king learned of his careless deed, made him fall to his knees.

Cam lowered his head to avoid Melikar's displeased scrutiny. "Master, you must punish me. You've been good to take me in, give me bread to eat, and a cot on which to sleep. Then I repay you with disobedience. I don't deserve to be your apprentice."

The wizard placed a hand upon Cam's shoulder. "Your prank was a thoughtless one, but the tapestry has been woven and the thread, snipped."

Melikar tightened his grip to quell his anger. "You weren't taken with Quinn because you weren't beneath the pool when the spell was cast. Once I've spoken the words allowing her to return, she must be standing atop the footbridge, directly over the pool.

"She must wish with all her heart to come home, then pivot to set the whirlpool in motion — the same way you created one by stirring the liquid in the cauldron. As the water begins to whirl, she will be drawn into it — as long as she doesn't resist the magic."

Melikar released his hold on Cam. "That is the only way Mandria's princess can return to her kingdom."

"She'll come back," Cam said, more to reassure

himself than Melikar. "She may explore a little first, but — "

"This is what I fear." Melikar studied the pool, but nothing was discernible through the now cloudy water. "The spell to return can be cast but once, and is strong for a quarter-moon's turn."

Cam's breathing stopped with the wizard's words. "That's only a few days."

The wizard's answer was a solemn nod.

The apprentice came to his feet. If he hadn't acted so rashly, he would have read all this in the _Book_ and discussed it fully with Quinn before impulsively whisking her out of Mandria.

Melikar moved to the stand that held the _Book_. Caressing the cover as though it were a favored child, he opened it gently. "I've been wise not to let you touch this. I trusted you were ready, but you've shown me it's still too soon."

Cam felt as disheartened as he had on the day he'd asked Melikar about his parents, and learned he'd been abandoned — left to be raised by the wizard.

He was a nobody, without a past — and with little promise for a future as an enchanter if he was never allowed to open the _Mandrian Book of Magic_.

It seemed he spent all his time trying to prove he was responsible — to earn Melikar's trust and

Quinn's affection. But if mistakes were gold pieces, he would truly be a wealthy lad.

The ring.

The question of why he'd appeared here instead of in the Marnies' candle chamber suddenly became clear to him. He'd been thinking of Quinn.

So. There was nothing wrong with the spell he'd cast on the ring; it was *his* fault. He supposed if Quinn had been in the candle chamber, he might have been more successful.

Melikar moved to his workbench as though the weight of both worlds was on his shoulders. He gathered a clean bowl and flask. "Fetch me a dish of queen of the meadow, prickly ash bark, doleran seeds — "

Cam's gasp caused the wizard to pause. "But sire, doleran seeds will stop a . . . a life."

"Not a life, lad. Time. The seeds, steeped in the royal afternoon tea, will make time stand still for the king and queen until their daughter's return. *If* she returns." He muttered the last part under his breath, but the words burned Cam's ears.

Heart pounding, the apprentice searched the oak cabinet for doleran seeds. *How can Melikar chance something like this?*

As if he'd read Cam's thoughts, Melikar replied, "Do you have a better course of action? If King Marit discovers his beloved daughter and only heir to the throne is missing on my account, he'll have both our heads."

Cam swallowed hard. The wizard had spoken the truth. A reply wasn't necessary.

Besides, hearing Melikar take the blame made Cam feel even worse. Meekly he asked, "Is there anything else we can do?"

The wizard's eyes suddenly dimmed to a watery red. "I will search the _Book_ for any spell I can cast from under the river to ensure Quinn's safety should she rashly decide to remain in the outer world."

3

The Other Side

In her dream, Quinn lifted the lace skirt of her gown and stepped down the spiral rock stairway from Melikar's chamber to the tunnels of Mandria.

Rushing along the main avenue, she followed its winding curves through the kingdom, dodging horse-drawn carriages full of visiting dignitaries.

Shops along the way glowed in the Marnies' warm candlelight — a dim imitation of the brightness she'd glimpsed above the wishing pool.

The dream journey took her to Ameka's cottage.

Her tutor wasn't home.

Suddenly panicked at being completely alone, the princess pounded on the cottage door, shouting for Ameka.

Quinn's eyes flew open.

Instantly she blinked them shut.

The brightness of the fiery sun was remarkably intense. Cupping one hand over her eyes, she sat up, squinting into the glow, feeling its warmth for the very first time.

Dizziness filled her head, making her feel as though she'd just danced the quick-stepping volta in the palace ballroom with her cousin, Dagon.

Quinn steadied herself, peering at her surroundings in spite of the painful brightness in her eyes.

Where was she?

Cam must have. . . . No, he couldn't have.

Suddenly she realized what she was sitting on. A curved wooden footbridge. Under the bridge, blue-green water sparkled in the light, like jewels in her father's crown.

Quinn caught her breath. The pool was _below_ her! Cam did it!

Her heart soared. _For once his magic worked!_

Scrambling to her feet, the princess felt as excited as she had the first time she'd been allowed to visit Melikar's chamber — and had caught her earliest glimpse of the world above the river.

Cam must have sent her up through the water, yet her gown wasn't wet — wasn't even damp.

She placed a hand to her head, trying to recall what had happened.

All she remembered was being drawn to the pool.

The tingling sensation had swept over her with such force, its subtle beckoning had become an urgent pull.

She'd heard Cam chant. Then an earthquake had rumbled through her head. What happened after that was hazy.

Cam. Where *was* he?

Quinn pivoted, searching for the apprentice. He was nowhere in sight. Was he playing tricks on her? Now was *not* the time for such foolishness.

"Cam?" she called. Her voice sounded weak and thin in this wide openness, without walls and tunnels to echo it back to her.

She stood transfixed, captivated by the scene that had always been out of her view from under the river.

No outer-earth folk were in sight. Still, Quinn hurried off the footbridge and into the dark forest, just to be safe. Here, shade from the great trees was much easier on her eyes.

Now the only thing to do was find a good sitting spot and wait for Cam to appear.

He *had* to, she told herself. She'd heard him say *both* their names when the spell was cast.

Inhaling one long breath after another, Quinn wandered into the forest, sampling fragrances all new to her.

Finding a boulder within clear view of the footbridge, she sat to think things over. If Cam *didn't* appear, surely Melikar would materialize in a lightning flash on top of the footbridge, robes flapping about him like wings, and rescue her.

As excited as she was about being in this world, the fearful fluttering of her heart told her she didn't want to miss what might be her only chance to return to Mandria.

Minutes passed. Nothing happened.

Quinn recalled Melikar's warning: _Outer earth isn't safe for enchanted beings._ Luckily or unluckily, she was an ordinary, unenchanted princess.

"Well, I'm where I wanted to be, but Cam's not here," she said out loud. Now her voice sounded small and trembly. She and Cam had always planned on taking this adventure together. Neither had suggested she do it by herself.

A foggy remembrance of her dream journey to Ameka's cottage washed over her. Was it truly a dream? Or a forewarning?

Panic returned in a rush. In Mandria, she was rarely alone — not with two ladies attending her, and Ameka taking up the rest of her time.

Quinn hugged herself, wishing she'd brought along a shawl. Her gown was no protection from the cool breeze. "I'm all alone," she whispered.

"I'm here," came a tiny voice from behind.

Quinn leaped to her feet. All she saw was an ancient tree with gold and red leaves rustling in the breeze. "Who's there?" She twisted her braid through her fingers, taking a wary step backward.

"Me. . . ."

The misty form of a young maiden, no taller than a Marnie's knee, shifted like a candle flame in front of the tree trunk.

Quinn caught her breath. Hadn't Melikar said all magical creatures lived underground?

"Are you an enchantress?" the wispy maiden asked. "Hundreds of years ago, we could move and talk, but when magic left the earth, we became still and mute. But you — " She pointed at Quinn. "You're surrounded with magic."

Fascinated, Quinn knelt for a better look. The outline of the maiden's smoky form was hazy. "No, I'm not an enchantress. Magic is common where I live, and — "

The princess stopped, remembering her promise to keep Mandria a secret. "Um, perhaps a little has rubbed off on me."

Another form appeared, floating above a lily of the valley like a wisp of steam.

Tiny maidens emerged one by one from the plants and trees nearest her. The moment she walked away, Quinn knew they'd disappear into their living homes.

"I can't make it last," she told them. "I'm sorry."

Remembering who she was, the princess returned to her rock throne, straightening the torn lace on her skirt. She was here as an ambassador from her kingdom; she must act accordingly.

"Who are you?" she asked the maidens. "And why weren't you taken when magic left the earth?"

"We're dryads," answered the figure by the oak tree. "Wood nymphs. Moving to the underground kingdoms was impossible because our homes are here. Melikar had to leave us behind."

"*Melikar?*" Hearing the wizard's name startled Quinn so much, she sprang to her feet. "How do you know of Melikar?"

The nymphs old enough to remember told Quinn of the time when earth was filled with magical creatures. They told how men began to capture spirits, turning good magic into evil, taking power for their own greedy intentions.

After a time, earth was no longer safe for anyone possessing the gift. So the great Melikar, enchanter of all enchanters, found a new world for his followers. And, without the surrounding magic, nymphs remained frozen in their forest homes.

Although the tale was quite absorbing, Quinn's attention kept wandering. She could not sit still and waste another moment. A whole world was waiting for her. And she'd better act now before Melikar called her home.

Bidding the maidens good-bye — and apologizing for taking away the magic — she hurried back to the footbridge. Leaning against the handrail, she gazed into the wishing pool.

Looking *down* into the water seemed odd after looking *up* through it all her life. Craning her neck, she searched for a glimpse of Melikar's chamber, but saw nothing more than her own reflection.

Something glinted in the sparkling water. Hoping it was a sign from below, Quinn dropped to her knees.

Cam's ring! Caught on the lacy hem of her gown! Pulling it free, she slipped the ring onto the middle finger of her right hand. It must have snagged on her dress when she collided with him.

The sudden sound of voices met her ears. Quinn's attention was drawn across a narrow clearing where the forest began. Outer-earth folk were coming down the path!

Hurrying off the footbridge, she gathered her full skirts and jumped onto the bank of the Mandrian River, hunching out of sight beneath the curve of the bridge.

"Hurry, Sarah!" shouted a young lad. "It's almost time for the shuttle to leave."

Quinn peeked.

A maiden about her age ran onto the bridge. Closing her eyes, she mumbled softly to herself.

Quinn tried so hard to get a good look, she almost splashed into the water. The maiden's fair hair was shorter than a lad's, which made the princess wrinkle her nose. What an oddity. Maidens in Mandria never cut their hair until they married. It was a Mandrian truth.

Her clothes were unusual, too: a buttonless shirt with writing on the front, and dark leggings like a lad would wear. Trinkets dangled from each ear. Quinn was fascinated and wanted to speak to her. Something about the maiden seemed familiar.

An old man broke through the bushes, stopping next to the lad. "Sarah!" he called. "Come away from the pool!"

The abrupt shout in the quiet forest made the maiden jump. Reaching deep into her pocket, she pulled out a coin, kissed it, then tossed it into the wishing pool.

Quinn imagined Melikar exclaiming, "Devil dust!" as the coin plunked to the floor of his chamber.

The maiden, Sarah, glanced in Quinn's direction. Quinn *did* recognize her. She was the one who'd upset Melikar by wishing for beauty.

Quinn thought her a bit plain, especially without billowing yards of hair. Still, she was pleasant-looking. Why such a wish?

The lad bounded onto the footbridge. He was taller than Sarah, with the same coloring.

Quinn's heart quickened. He was as handsome as any knight in Mandria. He even reminded her a little of Dagon.

"Come on, Sis. We'll miss the bus if you don't hurry. Mondo has to get home in time for work."

"But we just got here," she argued. "Why are we leaving already?"

The lad shrugged. "I don't know. Wondered the same thing myself."

Together they started toward the path through the forest where the old man waited.

Quinn's curiosity overflowed like the marble fountains on the castle green.

Scrambling onto the footbridge, she threw a final, hasty glance at the wishing pool — and home — then followed the strangers down the wooded path.

4

Dragons, Large and Small

Quinn kept her distance from the others on the path.

Whenever she slowed, a tingling shivered through her. Was the surrounding magic awakening other wood nymphs in the forest?

Hurrying on, she felt an unexplainable obsession to keep Sarah, the lad, and the old man in view.

The path ended.

Quinn came to an abrupt stop, staying in the shadowed trees for cover.

Dozens of outer-earth folk filled an open area, moving noisily around the strangest contraptions she'd ever seen.

One gigantic sphere held many swings filled with people. The circle turned, carrying swings high into the air, around, down, then up again.

Another looked like a giant spider, but at the end of each skinny leg was a spinning basket, also full of outer-earth folk.

Screams shook the air. Why were these people being punished?

Quinn's fear made her shrink further into the shelter of surrounding branches. This must be an outer-earth prison. How barbaric! In Mandria the worst punishments were life in a cold, dark dungeon, banishment, or a death sentence. They'd done away with torture such as this centuries ago.

It was a Mandrian truth.

Shuddering, her gaze traveled the crowd, watching for Sarah.

There she was. Climbing aboard another strange machine with large wheels. Worry over losing sight of the family was greater than Quinn's fear of being seen.

Catching up her skirts, she ran past a line of prisoners, hoping no one would mistake her for one of them.

Quinn hesitated a few steps from the monster who swallowed Sarah. It grumbled and belched dark smoke.

Its hunched form reminded Quinn of the great dragons that once roamed this world. Some still bothered the underground kingdoms. Now, small Mandrian dragons, quick to tame, were fashionable as pets.

Scrabit, her own pet dragon, had come as a birth gift from Sir Exeter, Lord of Chelwick. She and Scrabit had grown up together.

She loved dragons — small and tame — but didn't want her journey to end by being swallowed by one.

Don't be foolish, her mind chided. _It's not a dragon._

I know. But it's big and noisy, and it frightens me.

Sarah was watching her from inside the monster. The maiden didn't appear frightened at all.

"Are ya gittin' on or not?" came a gruff voice.

Quinn flinched at the rude comment directed at her by a burly man. No one _ever_ spoke to her like that. She was royalty. The man should have been whisked off to the dungeon by palace guards.

Or, _would_ have been if this were Mandria.

Taking a deep breath, Quinn caught hold of a handrail and pulled herself up the steps. Facing the outer-earth folk, she stared at them as they stared back at her.

The gruff man followed her up the stairs and sat behind a large wheel. "Take a seat; it's time to leave."

His nasty tone angered her. She glared at him, then realized he must be the prison guard. Better not vex him.

"Move!" he snapped.

Quinn repressed the urge to reprimand him, fearing

he might force her onto one of the torture contraptions. Lifting her chin, she proudly returned everyone's stares as she made her way between the rows of chairs in a grand fashion.

The old man was sitting next to the lad. Behind them sat Sarah. Quinn chose the empty seat next to her.

"Hi," the girl said, unable to take her eyes off Quinn's gown.

Before the princess could return the greeting, the dragon let out a great roar, then crept forward. Quinn braced herself, waiting for it to spin around, turn upside down, or make her scream.

The dragon simply moved faster.

"Are you okay?" the maiden asked, still gaping at her.

The dragon passed under a giant arch: YOU ARE NOW LEAVING WONDERLAND PARK. Quinn leaned toward the window to take it all in. "I'm fine, Sarah, thank you."

Sarah gave a little gasp. "How did you know my name?"

"I overheard your brother calling you."

"Adam?"

At the mention of his name, Adam rose up in the seat in front of her and leaned his elbows against the headrest.

His eyes quickly took in her face, her hair, and her gown. He offered his hand. "Hi. I'm Adam Dover."

Quinn didn't know what she was supposed to do, so she crooked her wrist and took hold of his fingers, expecting him to bow and kiss her hand. "I-I'm Quinn," she replied, feeling shy under his scrutiny.

"Quinn what?" He wiggled her hand up and down instead of kissing it.

How odd! How disrespectful! Had outer-earth folk never been in the presence of royalty?

"Quinn of Mandria," she replied, realizing they couldn't guess her nobility by her tattered appearance — and to tell them would endanger her secret.

Adam cocked his head, puzzled by her answer. Letting go of her hand, he motioned toward the man. "This is our grandfather, Mondo. We live with him."

Mondo turned, peering at her between the seats with a somber look. "Hello, Quinn." He spoke in a hushed voice, as if he didn't want others to hear. "Welcome."

The old man's face startled her.

His gaze was intense. His eyes, a vivid blue-green, the same deep hue as the wishing pool. The contrast of the color against his white hair and beard was striking.

A vague familiarity touched her senses. Had they met before?

And why had he greeted her with *"Welcome"*?

5

Puzzlements and Bewilderments

"The dress!" Sarah exclaimed, snapping her fingers. "I just figured out why you're dressed like that. You must be acting in the Shakespeare Festival at Wonderland Park."

The maiden grinned at Quinn, looking pleased with her conclusion. "Are you a princess?"

The question caught Quinn by surprise. "Why, yes." She dropped her voice. "How did you know?" Maybe it *was* obvious.

"By your costume." Sarah looked at Quinn as though her question were foolish. "Acting in a play must be really cool."

Quinn nodded. She had no idea what Sarah was talking about, or why an actor might be colder than anyone else.

Her attention was drawn beyond the maiden to the passing scenery.

The forest gave way to tall castles and cottages, but they were boxy and plain. No turrets. No towers. No drawbridges over moats.

If outer-earth folk lacked magic, they also lacked imagination.

The sun was low in the sky now, causing odd-shaped shadows to fall across the land. Lights appeared in a multitude of windows. Quinn wondered how large the candle chamber must be to supply all those candles. And who made them? All Marnies lived underground.

As they neared a giant kingdom, hundreds of strange-looking carriages filled the road. And they moved without horses!

Quinn even caught a glimpse of the flying machines Melikar had told her and Cam about.

And flying animals. Mandria had plenty of bats, mostly a bother, but these were cute and feathery, darting here and there.

Adam stepped into the aisle and leaned against the seat, facing the princess. He had the same blond hair as Sarah, and blue-green eyes like Mondo's, only not as intense.

Quinn fidgeted under his gaze, wondering why

he made her heartbeat lift the way it did whenever she raced the Mandrian tunnels on her pony, Trinka.

The lad's face was creased in curiosity, as if trying to solve a puzzle. "Where are you from?" he asked.

"Mandria."

"I thought that was your last name."

Weren't people here identified by their homeland?

Adam tilted his head, looking skeptical. "Is Mandria a suburb?"

She nodded, pretending to understand.

"So where are you going?"

"Um, to the kingdom." She waved her hand toward the tall buildings, wishing she knew what the kingdom was called.

"Kingdom," Adam repeated, chuckling. "Still playing the role of princess, are you? We peasants prefer to call it the city."

Quinn glanced at him. Adam certainly didn't look as tattered and thin as a Mandrian peasant boy.

"Why didn't you change out of your costume?" He pointed at her gown. "You're bound to attract attention dressed like that." Not waiting for an answer, he gave her another perplexed look, and returned to his seat.

Attract attention. That's exactly what she *didn't* want. Quinn glanced at the other travelers. Adam was right, she *did* look terribly out of place. She'd better dress like outer-earth folk if she wanted to fit in.

But how could she barter for clothes? She had nothing of value — except Cam's ring — and it might appear worthless to people here.

Feeling self-conscious, Quinn fussed with her full skirts, trying to fold them so they weren't so noticeable. She was ashamed of her torn, soiled gown.

Her appearance would mortify the queen. She would chasten Quinn's ladies (never the princess) for not properly attending to her daughter.

Quinn's heart lurched at the thought of her parents. Who would they blame tonight when she didn't attend the evening feast? She hoped her ladies kept their wits about them, and made excuses for her until she returned.

They'd covered for her in the past when she'd lost track of time during visits with Melikar, the Marnies, or when she and Ameka were off in a distant part of the kingdom.

Uneasiness settled over her as daylight dipped into evening. She was traveling far from the wishing pool — and home — with no idea where she was going. How would she ever find her way back to Mandria?

Why am I so impulsive? Quinn bit her lip, chastising herself.

She always assumed any adventure she might have in this world would take place near the wishing pool. Why had she been so drawn to follow the Dover family?

Her troubled feeling soared into panic. It was almost feast time. Where would she stay the night? Why hadn't Cam given her fair warning?

If they'd planned this venture in advance, she would have brought a change of gowns, one of her ladies, and gold pieces for food and lodging at an inn.

Mondo had seemed friendly, but how could she tell him she needed assistance? He was a stranger. Could she trust him?

As if he'd read her mind, Mondo turned to speak to her. "In a few minutes, we'll be stopping at our car. Come with us, Quinn. You will be our guest while you're visiting the city." He touched two fingers to his right cheek, making the sign of a backward seven.

"What?" yelped Sarah. "She's not visiting the city. She's just going home on the shuttle." Sarah faced her. "Aren't you?"

Quinn didn't answer. Her gaze remained fixed on the old man.

He'd given her the sign of the Lorik! An ancient Mandrian sign of trust and secrecy. Those who shared the sign shared a bond that could not be broken. It was one of the highest Mandrian truths.

Quinn now knew what she'd already sensed. She could trust Mondo completely. Her hand trembled as she lifted it to her cheek to return the Lorik sign.

Mondo continued as if nothing unusual had transpired between them. "Sarah will lend you some of her clothes."

"What?" Sarah made a _tsking_ sound as though offended at not being consulted. She gave Quinn a sidelong frown. "Do you go to Caprock High? I've never seen you there, and I'm _sure_ I'd remember someone with hair as long as yours."

"Um, no," Quinn stammered. _Caprock High_? "I truly _am_ here on a visit." She hoped her words sounded convincing.

Everything was happening too fast. She'd _meant_ to come to this world as an _observer_. Her mind blurred with visions of staying with this family and wearing Sarah's clothes.

"Wait a minute." Adam wrinkled his brow in confusion. "Your parents let you visit the city alone? And you're traveling without luggage or regular clothes?" He glanced suspiciously from his grandfather to Quinn. "What's going on? This doesn't make sense."

"Are you a runaway?" Sarah blurted. "Are you hiding from the law?"

The law? Why is she wishing the worst for me?

"Enough, you two," Mondo ordered. "Be patient. When we get home, Quinn will tell you who she *really* is and will answer all your questions."

"What?!" Quinn felt faint. "But I can't . . . how did you . . . ?"

Before she could put her shock into words, the dragon — or *shuttle* as Sarah had called it — pitched forward and stopped.

Quinn peered out the window. They were in a field full of horseless carriages. Sarah nudged her into line with the other travelers, so she followed them outside.

As Adam and Sarah climbed into one of the small carriages, Mondo pulled her aside.

"My child," he whispered, "I know of Mandria. You must give me your complete trust."

He placed a hand on her shoulder, then quickly withdrew it. So. He knew the rules of royal protocol.

"It's imperative that you stay with us while you're here," Mondo added. "Our meeting at the wishing pool was not by chance."

Did the wizard have something to do with this? Quinn wondered. Did he hold power in *both* worlds?

Mondo hurried on before she could respond. "I don't have time to answer questions now. But you *must* tell Adam and Sarah the truth. I give you my solemn pledge your secret will be safe with them."

Again he touched two fingers to his cheek.

Uncertainty tightened Quinn's throat. How could she return the sign? Not when he was asking her to break her vow to Melikar. How could she reveal the secret of her kingdom?

"Melikar has spoken," the old man whispered.

Hearing the wizard's name caused her heart to falter. Yet, those were precisely the words Quinn needed to hear.

With a shaking hand, she returned the sign of the Lorik.

6
Telling the Secret

Mondo steered the carriage a short distance, stopping in front of a row of identical cottages, one piled on top of the other. "Go inside and make Quinn feel at home while I'm at work," he said.

The instant Mondo disappeared, Adam and Sarah rained a multitude of questions upon their guest.

Weary from all the excitement and turmoil of her sojourn, Quinn stopped them. "Can't we go inside your cottage first?"

"Cottage?" Sarah smirked. "Try apartment."

Quinn didn't like the way Sarah made her feel foolish each time she spoke. Maybe after everything was explained, the maiden would be more understanding.

They climbed a flight of stairs. Sarah unlocked the

door to one of the matching *apartments* with a key hanging from a chain around her neck.

They swept Quinn inside and onto a padded bench with stuffed cushions before she had a chance to view their home.

Furnishings under the river were mostly made of wood, but this chamber was filled with many kinds of materials and colors.

The setting was cozy, but Quinn puzzled over the instant light brightening the room when they entered. Nowhere did she see candles.

"Stop stalling," Sarah insisted, "and tell us who you *really* are."

Adam, who possessed more patience than his sister, passed around the bread and meat Mondo had purchased during the journey home.

Quinn settled herself onto the cushions, taking hungry bites of her evening feast, despite the worried knot in her stomach.

There was no getting around it. She had to trust Mondo's judgment and tell Adam and Sarah the truth.

Please don't let me endanger the secret of my kingdom, she prayed to the highest spirit.

Setting aside the food, Quinn straightened, still trying to look regal. Lifting her chin, she proclaimed,

"I am Princess Quinnella from the kingdom of Mandria."

The silence of their disbelief drifted across the room.

Were they waiting for her to laugh and say she was merely joking?

"You mean you're a *real* princess?" Sarah's voice overflowed with skepticism.

Quinn nodded, brushing away hair loosened from her braid.

"So where is your kingdom?" Adam asked.

The princess wasn't sure how to respond. "Under the river," was the best answer she could give.

Doubt clouded his eyes. "*What* river?"

"The Mandrian River. Where the wishing pool is."

Sarah's eyes lit up at the mention of the pool. "Oh, the wishing pool. I love it there; it's so peaceful."

"That's not the Mandrian River," Adam said. "It's the Canadian River. At least that's what *we* call it."

Sarah hugged her knees to her chest. "I go right to the wishing pool whenever Mondo takes us to Wonderland Park."

"I know," Quinn said. "You've wished for beauty."

The maiden gasped, shooting an embarrassed look at her brother. "How did you know that?"

"I've seen you — and heard you — from under the pool."

Silence.

Adam shoved away his dinner. "This is too weird."

"Weird is right." Sarah scooted to the opposite end of the padded bench — away from Quinn.

The princess doubted they'd believe the rest of her story, but she'd promised Mondo. . . .

Taking a deep breath, she told them about her life under the river, describing the castle, the Marnies, Melikar.

They listened intently, as though she were telling a bedtime fable.

"Now it's *your* turn," she finished, anxious to change the subject. Melikar's fear that outer-earth folk might discover the existence of Mandria made her not want to say too much. "Tell me about Mondo."

"What's to tell?" Adam said. "He's our grand-father."

"How does he know of Mandria?"

Adam looked at his sister and shrugged.

"We don't know," Sarah said. "He's never mentioned it to us."

"But we haven't known him very long," her brother added. "Mondo came here as our only living relative after our parents died in a car accident two years ago. He became our legal guardian."

Quinn had wondered about their parents, but felt it wasn't proper to ask.

"Dad used to talk about Mondo," Sarah said. "But he never knew where Mondo was." The maiden's voice trembled when she mentioned her father. "Our grandmother died before we were born, and afterward, according to Dad, it was too hard for Mondo to stay here, so he left."

"We don't know *how* he heard about our parents' accident," Adam told her, "but he came for us right away, got a job as a cabinetmaker, moved us into this apartment, and here we are."

Quinn's heart went out to them over the sadness they'd endured. Still, she wondered about Mondo's connection to Mandria.

Sarah began to chuckle. "Wait till the kids at school hear — "

"No!" Quinn's earlier feeling of panic gripped her again. "Mondo *promised* you'd keep my secret."

Sarah made a face, looking disappointed.

Adam nudged his sister. "Sary, you can't tell anyone. Who would believe you, anyway?"

She shrugged.

"It might put Quinn in danger if anyone found out," he said. "Promise you won't tell?"

Sarah nudged him back. "You're taking all the fun out of it."

"Adam is right," Quinn told her. "You *must* keep this an absolute secret." She taught them the sign of the Lorik and explained what it meant. "It's a Mandrian truth," she whispered.

"You don't have to whisper." Sarah still looked peeved at not being allowed to talk about the princess who'd come to visit.

"I don't want the servants to hear," Quinn said.

"Servants?" Adam laughed. "There must be lots of differences between our worlds. I think you might need a private tutor while you're here." He stood and bowed with a flourish. "Allow me to instruct you, O beautiful princess."

Quinn felt herself blushing. Did he truly think she was beautiful?

She'd never thought so. Her nose was slightly crooked from the time Scrabit darted in front of Trinka, sending her tumbling from the pony's saddle. And her eyelashes were so pale they could barely be seen.

Quinn glanced at the magic ring on her finger. Could she wish for beauty? Like Sarah?

The memory of Melikar's disgust over trivial wishes was her answer. *"Magic is mighty,"* he'd said. *"And must be used for mighty purposes."*

Sarah acted annoyed by her brother's attentiveness toward Quinn. "Are you going to school with us tomorrow?" she demanded in a clipped tone.

"I-I don't know." The idea hadn't occurred to her, but it was intriguing. "Perhaps, I will."

"Well, I'd better lay out clothes for you because you can't show up at Caprock High wearing a medieval gown."

Sarah rose, grabbing her untouched meal and drink. "I guess you'll have to sleep in my room. There's an extra bed in there for *invited* guests."

Quinn didn't miss the sarcasm. Why was Sarah so unfriendly? All the maidens in Mandria were at Quinn's beck and call. No one *ever* talked back, much less insulted her.

She bit her lip, resisting the urge to lecture Sarah on proper behavior in the presence of royalty. Why should *she* care if Sarah liked her? Besides, the kingdom of Mandria would continue to exist whether or not this silly maiden believed in it.

Quinn watched Sarah disappear down a tunnel in the apartment. She'd best keep peace, especially if she had to depend on the maiden while attending lessons with her.

Adam sprawled on the floor, studying Quinn with an intensity that made her nervous. Suddenly a kitten with orange and white fur tore through the chamber and sprang onto Quinn's lap, startling her.

She reached a timid hand to pet him. Cats were

rare in Mandria, but lived for hundreds of years. Marnies were the sole keepers of cats.

Adam chuckled at her reaction. "This is Katze. My German teacher gave him to me. *Katze* is the German word for *cat*."

"German?" Quinn felt more comfortable asking Adam questions. He didn't make her feel foolish the way Sarah did.

"Um." He paused to raise an eyebrow. "The language spoken in Germany?"

"Oh." The knowledge that everyone in this world did not speak the same language surprised her.

"Wow," he said. "I think being your tutor will keep me *busy*."

Quinn laughed, leaning against the cushions. The tension cramping her neck had disappeared the moment Sarah left the room. Why did Adam accept her, yet his sister refused?

He grabbed Katze off Quinn's lap and wrestled with him on the floor. "Tell me about school in Mandria."

"I don't go to school."

"You don't? Why not?"

"In Mandria, I really *do* have a tutor. Her name is Ameka."

Adam looked impressed.

Quinn hadn't meant to sound boastful. "I *am* a princess," she reminded him.

"How could I forget?" he teased. "Look at you."

He cocked his head. "If you don't go to school, then you probably don't go to dances."

"Oh, we have many balls at the castle."

"Do you dance?"

"Of course. It's part of a princess's instruction on being a lady."

"Being a lady? Sounds pretty weird in this day and age." Adam patted Katze away and leaned against the cushioned bench. "Who do you dance with at the balls?"

"Cam and Dagon, but I'm required to dance with sons of visiting dignitaries."

"Are Cam and Dagon your boyfriends?"

"My what?"

"Your . . . um, what would you call them? Your admirers? Your suitors?"

Adam's questions made her uneasy. "No. Dagon is my cousin, and Cam . . . Cam is Melikar's apprentice." She twisted her braid through her fingers. "Cam doesn't come from nobility, so he cannot be a proper suitor."

"A proper suitor," Adam repeated.

Her face grew warm. "Why are you asking all these questions?"

He pushed himself from the floor to sit beside her.

"I want to warn you —" He paused, as though choosing his words with care. "_If_ you decide to go to classes with Sarah, the _minute_ you step into school, a million guys are going to fall at your feet."

She was flattered. "Why would they bow before me? They won't know I'm royalty — unless you tell them, and you promised you wouldn't."

Adam ran his fingers through his close-cropped hair. "Let me rephrase that. You will definitely attract a lot of attention from the guys."

"Why?" The kitten sprang back into her lap and began to purr. Quinn wondered why she'd always feared these harmless pets.

"Because you're different," Adam said. "You _look_ different, you _talk_ different, your skin is so incredibly pale, it's like a . . . a white sheet of paper. And your hair." He took hold of her braid, pulling it in front of her shoulder. "Your hair is fantastic. No girl at school has hair this long."

Adam dropped her braid, averting his eyes. "Sorry. Guess I got carried away."

He fell silent for a moment, turning back to stare at her.

Quinn loved gazing into his eyes. It made her feel dizzy.

"I guess what I'm trying to say is —" He rose to

pace across the chamber. "Will you go to the Halloween dance with me this weekend? If I don't ask you now, somebody else will beat me to it."

Quinn's heart fluttered. Adam was asking to court her!

In Mandria, it wasn't proper to court a princess until she was sixteen. And Adam would need to ask the king's permission — a task certain to scare off even the most serious suitor.

But this wasn't Mandria. This was another world, and all Quinn had to answer was . . . "Yes."

Then worry struck her. What if there were certain *rules* for courting, like in Mandria? Rules she didn't know about. Surely Adam would instruct her, wouldn't he?

"Great!" was all he said. He stopped pacing and sat beside her.

"Adam?"

"Yes."

"What is Halloween?"

He laughed. "Good thing you have a tutor nearby. But you'll see for yourself in a few days."

A few days. It sounded like a long time for her to be away from home. Was it wise? Melikar and Cam were probably beside themselves with worry.

Her heart pounded as she thought of her parents. Surely Melikar could keep them calm. Couldn't he?

Oh, bother.

Too many worries whirled through her head.

Quinn sighed. She was getting drowsy. Maybe if she stayed one night and went to lessons tomorrow, she'd learn all she wanted to about this world and be ready to go home.

Adam's nearness made her feel even dizzier. He stroked her cheek with the back of his hand. Though not used to being touched by anyone besides her ladies, she welcomed his gentle caress and the warmth it cascaded through her.

Quinn met his eyes. Would it be proper to ask Adam to hug her the way couples on the footbridge hugged? Was it unprincesslike to request such a thing? Adam would be the perfect one to show her.

He was so close, she could sense his heartbeat.

Part of her wanted the moment to last forever, and part of her wished she was in Sarah's sleeping chamber in bed.

Tingles skittered down her spine. The chamber pitched into blackness. Pounding hooves stampeded through her head, then stillness claimed her.

Quinn opened her eyes.

Sarah stood over her, eyes wide, mouth gaping.

Running footsteps sounded nearby.

"Sary!" Adam shouted. "She disappeared!"

He burst through the door. "She dis — !" The sight of Quinn stopped him. "What *happened?*"

Shaken, the princess sat up. She was in Sarah's sleeping chamber in bed.

Lifting her trembling hand, she showed them Cam's ring. "I guess its magic works in both worlds. I'd better be careful what I wish."

The flicker of doubt she'd seen earlier in Sarah's eyes was gone. In one instant display of magic, she'd earned Sarah's belief — as well as Adam's, had he any misgivings.

"What *else* can you do with the ring?" Sarah asked, flopping onto the foot of the bed. "Show us more magic!"

The princess untangled her braid from the bed covers. "I can't."

"Why not?" they asked in unison.

"Because Melikar allows no one to use magic lightly — especially for amusement. It's a Mandrian truth."

Sarah frowned. "Qui-inn, come on, do something else."

Quinn lay back, yanking a quilt over her head. Why all this fuss over a little magic? If they'd seen *half* the magic she'd seen in Mandria —

Sarah jerked away the quilt. "Melikar's not here," she persisted. "And — "

A sharp ringing interrupted Sarah's plea, making Quinn's heart leap inside her chest.

Was it a sign from the wizard telling her he *was* here? Hovering invisibly in this world? Keeping an eye on her to make sure she upheld all Mandrian truths?

Adam reached for something on the dresser and held it to his ear. He said a few words, then set the object down. "That was Mondo. He wanted to make sure everything was all right."

Now it was Quinn's turn to be stunned. "But I thought magic was *gone* from this world."

They laughed instead of answering.

Adam gave a tired sigh. "I think I have a full day of tutoring ahead, so I'll say good-night. My brain's had all it can handle with underground kingdoms and disappearing princesses."

After he left, Sarah climbed into bed without saying another word.

Quinn pulled herself from under the quilt. She'd never prepared for sleep by herself. Her ladies always turned down the bed, warmed it, then helped her out of her gown and unbraided her hair.

Removing the gown by herself was not easy with all the tiny buttons lining the back from her neck to hips. She draped the dress over a chair, feeling modest about disrobing in front of Sarah, who'd laid out a nightgown for her. Quinn slipped it on, then kicked off her jeweled Mandrian slippers.

Not bothering to unbraid her hair, Quinn returned to bed as the light mysteriously blinked out. She missed her nightly cup of tea, but wasn't about to ask Sarah to prepare a cup for her.

In the haze before sleep, Quinn wondered why the magic ring had worked when she hadn't twisted it three times. Maybe its enchantment was much more powerful than Cam knew.

Quinn thought of Melikar. Had he cast a spell from under the river to make sure she met the Dover family? Mondo had said their meeting was not by chance.

Conflicting feelings of comfort and uneasiness nudged her at the thought of Melikar tracking her sojourn on outer earth.

Did he know she possessed the ring, and had used its power — by accident? Would it anger him?

Closing her eyes in sleep, she vowed once more, *I'd better be careful what I wish.*

She hoped her good intentions reached the world below.

7
This World's Magic

Light from the sun glistened through the window, waking Quinn. Stretching, she marveled at being awakened by daylight.

What would she be doing right now in Mandria?

Her ladies-in-waiting would enter her chamber to light the candles. They'd fill her bath with heated water from one of the underground springs, lay out a fresh gown, and bring her a cup of hot ginger tea.

The ladies would help her dress and braid her hair. Then she'd join her parents in the dining hall for breakfast.

Afterward, they'd go their separate ways: the king to advisory sessions with his knights of counsel; the queen to meet with noble ladies of the court, planning Mandrian cultural events; and Quinn to her private tutor.

Ameka was seventeen, and though strict about Quinn minding her lessons, every once in a while she let the princess spend an afternoon visiting an unexplored corner of the kingdom.

Once they visited the Marnies' village to watch the carving of a wooden cabinet for Quinn's chamber.

Woodcarving was the Marnies' specialty. Wood was abundant in the kingdom, thanks to their method of burrowing up through the roots of trees, and removing the core in long sections. Next, they'd burrow beside the trunk and plant young saplings, sprouted beneath the ground, to replace the tree they'd taken.

A buzzer sounded, startling Quinn.

Sarah stirred, reaching toward a box near her bed. The buzzing stopped. "Time to get up," she said, yawning. "You can take a shower while I fix breakfast."

"Shower?" Quinn asked.

"Oh, I forgot." Sarah staggered out of bed and slipped into a gray robe. "Come on. I'll show you what a shower is." She paused. "You *do* know what breakfast is, don't you?"

Quinn smiled in answer as she got out of bed and padded barefoot down the hallway, pleased to find Sarah much nicer this morning.

Sarah unbraided Quinn's hair, fetched a towel, then turned on the shower.

The sight of water spraying from a wall astonished the princess. "Magic!" she exclaimed.

"Plumbing," Sarah answered. "Pretend it's rain."

"Rain?"

Sarah stopped. "You mean, you don't even know what rain is?"

"Whenever the wishing pool is riddled with drops of water, Melikar says it's raining in the other world."

Sarah pulled her robe tight. "Having you around will take some getting used to." She stepped from the room and closed the door.

Quinn's first shower was invigorating — especially with all the sweet smelling salves and soaps — but shampooing the many handfuls of her hair wasn't easy. Her ladies always did it for her.

Doing things herself made Quinn grateful for her ladies. Maybe she could surprise them with thank-you gifts from this world.

Untangling her wet hair, she attempted to braid it. After a frustrating few minutes, she gave up, letting it fall loose to the back of her knees. Not having her hair braided today was the *least* of her worries.

Quinn dressed in garments Sarah lent her, feeling strange in leggings and the green, oversized top.

Finding her way to the kitchen, she sat down to a breakfast of toast, eggs, and juice. Finally — a similarity between the two worlds.

Adam and Sarah were quiet this morning, although Adam kept staring at her. Mondo had worked late and was still asleep.

Quinn's apprehension over going to lessons with Sarah began to mount as the others prepared to leave. *Should I stay here?*

And miss the opportunity to experience a new world?

I know, she argued with her conscience, *but I feel safe here in the apartment.*

You'll never get another chance.

Quinn groaned. She hated it when her conscience reminded her that nothing new and different ever happened to her in Mandria.

Following Adam and Sarah outside and down the steps, she shaded her eyes from the brightness. A great yellow carriage hunched in front of the apartments.

"It's a school bus," Adam whispered as they boarded. He greeted his friends, then moved to a seat in the back. Quinn sat next to Sarah, and tried not to stare at those around her, although *they* were staring at her.

Sarah introduced her as Quinn Mandria, the Dovers' cousin.

Mondo had left a note for Sarah to give to the headmaster, saying Quinn's records were coming from a previous school.

He felt it would allow her a couple days' taste of lessons with few questions asked. The plan worried Quinn. She hoped it worked.

I'm staying for only one day, she reminded herself.

The princess fidgeted in her seat as the bus lumbered along a wide avenue. The brightness still bothered her eyes, and Sarah's clothes and jacket were uncomfortable. The shoes were strange, too. Made of canvas, they tied like a lad's.

Besides all that, her damp hair kept falling across her face.

Trying to look like an outer-earth maiden was *not* giving her the self-confidence she needed right now.

She wished the young folk would quit gaping at her. Was it her hair? Should she cut it short like Sarah's? But then the people of Mandria would stare when she returned.

Quinn glanced at Sarah. She looked striking today in a purple that set off her pale hair. She wore dangling purple trinkets from her ears, with matching bangles and rings.

Even her eyelids were purple. Quinn liked the way it looked and wondered how Sarah had done it.

The princess closed her eyes as a sudden dose of anxiety began to choke her. The reality of being in this world was overwhelming. She wasn't ready to rush madly into the unknown, yet that's exactly what she was doing.

Anxiety traded places with homesickness as memories of her parents came to mind. They must be terribly worried by now. She hadn't meant to upset them.

Quinn twisted the magic ring three times, wishing Melikar might cast a spell to keep the king and queen from fretting. Would the ring's magic reach all the way to the other world?

Anxiety returned, making it hard to breathe. Quinn pulled at the neck of her garment. *This isn't what I wanted. Cam is supposed to be with me. Exploring outer earth in secret. I don't want to be on a school bus, pretending to be somebody's cousin — somebody who doesn't even like me.*

Whatever had possessed her to attend lessons at all?

She'd rather be in Mandria, wearing her own clothes, reading for Ameka, pestering Melikar, playing with Scrabit, or arguing with Cam.

Imagining this world from under the river seemed a lot safer than being here. She had to get off the bus.

Quinn grabbed Sarah's arm. "This isn't going to work," she whispered. "I want to go home."

Disappointment touched Sarah's eyes, yet Quinn wondered if it stemmed more from losing the attention her unusual "cousin" was bringing, than from the princess actually going home.

"You can't leave now," Sarah told her. "You're just homesick. I was, too, when my parents died and we had to move out of our house."

Quinn was only half-listening. Was the wishing pool the only way to return to Mandria? Could she find it by herself? Why hadn't she paid more attention on the trip from Wonderland Park? "Sarah, you don't understand. I can't —"

Giving a sudden squeal, Sarah hushed her. "Here he comes!" she yelped. "Oh, he's looking right at us. Act natural."

A tall, brawny lad with dark hair and eyes had boarded the bus, and was sauntering down the aisle. He wore a short upper garment, exposing his midriff. On the garment was a large numeral.

Sarah giggled, acting nervous. "Hi, Zack," she said in a singsongy voice.

He stopped at their seat. "Hey, Sarah," he answered. "Who's this?" Taking hold of Quinn's chin, he jerked her face upward so he could get a better look at her.

Quinn bristled. No one in Mandria would dare such an action. He'd be banished from the kingdom — or worse. It was a Mandrian truth.

Quinn tried to pull away, but he tightened his grip. Voices quieted as everyone watched. She glared at him, wishing he'd let go of her.

A spark crackled between them. Zack jerked his hand away, as if stung by a scorpion. It happened too fast for anyone but them to notice.

"What the — ?" He rubbed his hand against his shirt, glancing at his audience, then muttered under his breath, "Who *are* you?"

"Oh, Zack, she's just my cousin," explained Sarah, rushing on, "How's football practice going?"

Quinn was thankful for Sarah's attempt to distract the lad, but his eyes never left her face. How could she be so foolish? Using magic on a stranger? Granted, it was an accident — yet he deserved it.

Quinn averted her eyes, hoping if she ignored him he'd leave. A coldness emanated from him, chilling her heart. A coldness she hadn't felt since she'd toured the dungeons of Mandria.

Disregarding Sarah, Zack leaned over Quinn, whis-

pering into her ear. "I'll see *you* later, little cousin."
His breath smelled like the spirits brewed by dwarfs
on the outskirts of Mandria.

Zack started to touch her hair, then hesitated. Pulling his hand away, he slid into the nearest seat.

Revulsion rolled over Quinn, making her ill.

Next to her, Sarah slumped in her seat, giggling.
"Isn't he the coolest guy you've ever seen?"

8

The Apprentice's Nightmare

Under the river, Cam woke, flinching from a worrisome dream.

The fire on the hearth was almost dead. He rose from the cot in his corner of Melikar's chamber, grabbed a candle, and held it close to the glowing embers until the wick burst into flame.

Shaking his head to hasten wakefulness, he wondered if his dream was *only* a dream — or a forewarning. Most dreams — to a wizard — were premonitions, yet being a mere apprentice, *his* were few and far between.

He *had* foretold the arrival of Dagon from Twickingham Castle, but Quinn insisted she'd mentioned the upcoming visit from her cousin — meaning *she'd* planted the image in Cam's mind, which ultimately spawned the dream.

Cam remembered the ensuing quarrel over whether he'd ever become a master wizard like Melikar, or if his powers would always be limited, due to his unknown heritage.

The apprentice sighed. He *missed* arguing with Quinn.

As for the question of his unknown heritage, he wished it would go away and leave him be.

Cam raised the candle to the hourglass on the wall. Twelve hours worth of sand had flowed through the glass, marking night's end. He'd overslept.

"Bats!" he cursed out loud. It was his duty to turn the hourglass over as the last few grains of sand trickled into the bottom half.

Cam turned the glass upside down, wondering how long he'd slept. He shook it to hurry ahead the sand, hoping to make up for the missed time.

Melikar was already gone. Cam moved about the chamber, lighting candles, rebuilding the fire. The wizard had been gone a lot lately, helping Marnies develop a new method of food production for the kingdom.

The old way called for Melikar to cast a daily spell in the food-growing chambers so brightness engulfed the room, allowing vegetables and fruits to grow.

But the Marnies had developed mutant seeds, which grew in dim candlelight, thus saving time and energy for Melikar, who could divert his attention to other matters.

Cam set the candle on the workbench, halfheartedly reaching for a broom to sweep up the latest coins rained from above.

He collected them into a pile, wondering if he should gather the useless coins in a basket and cast the spell he'd cast upon Quinn, sending the basket into the other world.

Surely the princess needed something of earthly value to barter for food and a place to lodge.

Quinn.

Cam could hardly bear to think about her. He recalled his last glimpse of the princess, waving goodbye from above the wishing pool.

After Melikar had cast the spell allowing her to return, Cam felt as if a load of firewood had been lifted from his shoulders.

But then, nothing happened.

Knowing Quinn, she'd chosen to remain in the outer world. But what if *now* she desired to come home?

Thanks to him, she didn't know how.

Cam missed her terribly and had lain on his cot, wishing as many times as there were grains of sand in the hourglass, he'd traveled to outer earth with her.

Was she safe? Where did she stay the night? Had she found food? Was she angry at him for sending her there? Or pleased with him for causing it?

Too many painful questions bothered his mind, making his heart catch in his throat.

Was she missing him, too?

Cam dropped to one knee, sweeping beneath a cabinet. The broom knocked against something. He reached under and pulled out the ladle, which had gone flying the moment he'd collided with Quinn.

He thought of the magic ring. Here was one place he'd forgotten to look. Thrusting his arm under the cabinet, he felt each corner.

The ring wasn't there. It wasn't *anywhere* he'd looked.

Did Quinn have it? Was it possible?

Cam set the broom by the hearth and returned to his cot. He was glad for Melikar's absence because he didn't feel like doing chores. Lying down, he closed his eyes to worry over the nightmare troubling his sleep.

In his dream, Quinn was in great danger. She was running through a forest. Tree branches reached out to her. Were they trying to harm or help her? He couldn't tell.

A young knave was chasing Quinn. He *did* mean her harm; Cam could feel it. He was tall and strapping, with dark hair and strange clothes. On the front of his tunic was a large numeral.

Cam wanted desperately to help the princess, but there was nothing he could do from under the river.

Closing his eyes, he slipped from pondering the dream into dreaming it. A knock brought him to his feet.

Shaking the nightmare from his mind, he moved to open the portal.

Ameka greeted him with a bright smile.

" 'Morning, Cam." Her skirts swished past him as she stepped into Melikar's chamber. Her simply styled, moss-green dress set off her eyes of the same hue, as well as her lengths of nutmeg tresses.

"Quinn is late for lessons this morning. When she's tardy, I always find her here, pestering Melikar." Her gaze darted about the chamber as she spoke. "Is she here?"

"Um . . . no," Cam stammered.

What should he tell her? Melikar had taken care that the king and queen not discover their daughter's disappearance, but he must have forgotten the royal tutor would likewise be looking for the princess.

"Do you know where she is?" Ameka asked.

The maiden was as tall as Cam, so it was hard to avoid meeting her gaze as she faced him. "Yes," he answered, offering no more.

"Where?" Curiosity glinted in her eyes.

Cam paused. He knew Melikar wanted Quinn's whereabouts kept secret, but Ameka would *have* to be told.

Touching two fingers to his cheek, he formed a backward seven, the sign of the Lorik.

The sign took Ameka by surprise, making her gasp. "Where *is* she? Is she in danger?"

He answered with silence.

"All right," she whispered, frowning in worry. "I pledge to keep your secret." She returned the Lorik sign. "Cam, this is serious. I have to answer to Queen Leah if Quinn misses a day of instruction."

"I know," he answered, sighing. "I'm not quite sure how to tell you."

"What? Is she down in the candle chamber? Riding Trinka? Off to the Marnies' village?" Worry clouded her eyes. "Oh, I hope she took Scrabit along for protection. Who knows what type of rogues might be out and about today."

Cam was having a hard time putting his answer into words. "The princess isn't anywhere, um, *below* us."

Ameka gave him a puzzled look. "Well, she *has* to be somewhere *below* us, because if she's somewhere *above*, she'd be — "

Cam nodded, watching surprise pale Ameka's face.

"She's on outer earth?"

He nodded again.

Ameka broke into excited laughter. "That's wonderful! How did she — ?"

Cam pointed to the wishing pool.

"The pool. Of course. Quinn is forever fascinated with the other world — and now the king and queen have let her go." Ameka rushed to the circle of light beneath the water, gazing upward. "Who escorted her?"

"No one," Cam answered in a grim voice. "And the king and queen don't know she's gone."

Ameka stared at the apprentice. Her smile faded.

Cam knew what she was thinking. No one deceived King Marit and lived to tell about it.

"That's frightful," Ameka whispered. "I trust this explains the secrecy?"

Cam told her the details, taking full blame, and mentioning the enchanted tea Melikar had given the king and queen to prevent them from knowing.

"In spite of the danger, I still can't help feeling excited for her." Ameka's slim frame twirled in the pool's circle of light.

"Stop!" Cam blurted, eyes transfixed on the water. He waited, feeling jumpy, but a whirlpool did *not* form.

Of course not, he told himself. He was getting the spell to return to Mandria mixed up with the spell to leave.

Ameka stared at him. "Cam, what's wrong?"

"Nothing." He felt foolish now. "I-I'd simply feel better if you stopped twirling."

Ameka obeyed, craning her neck to see as much as she could of outer earth from under the river. "Oh, I do hope she writes everything down — what she sees, hears, what she does." Stopping, she laughed at herself. "I sound like a tutor, don't I?"

Cam agreed, glancing at the now-inaccurate hourglass, hoping he wasn't late for his own lessons. Only royalty had the benefit of a private tutor. Melikar's influence had gotten him into lessons held for the sons of Mandria's nobility.

Ameka stayed beneath the pool, hands clasped as though she were praying. "Is there any way you might send Quinn a message with your magic? I mean, can you give her a mental hint to keep a written record of her travels? It would be so valuable to us here when she returns."

"I'll try," Cam promised. "Indeed, I will." He

chose not to mention the newest Mandrian truth. The princess didn't know *how* to return.

After Ameka departed, Cam quickly finished his morning chores.

He'd have to ask Melikar about conveying hints from one mind to another. When he and Quinn were younger, they played at sending each other silent messages, but it'd been a long time since he'd tried it.

However, he would oblige Ameka by trying it again — this time to ask Quinn to write of her sojourn on outer earth. Perhaps someday she'd allow him to read the account of who was chasing her through the forest — and how the chase ended.

Cam threw off the foreboding feeling his dream had given him.

Hurrying down the spiral rock steps to the tunnels of Mandria, he focused on the first *hint* he planned to send the princess:

Please come home; this lowly apprentice misses you. . . .

9

Beware of Potted Plants

Quinn stepped off the bus, raising her eyes to take in the great stone building before her. It was the closest thing to a castle she'd seen on outer earth — but was much more foreboding.

Still, it gave her a feeling of familiarity simply to look at it.

Adam gave her an encouraging wave before dashing off with his friends. Quinn hated to see him go. Why couldn't she attend classes with him instead of Sarah?

"This way." Sarah led her through large double doors. A crowd of noisy scholars shuffled down a dimly lit hall, which reminded Quinn of a Mandrian tunnel.

After checking in at the headmaster's chamber, and

leaving the note from Mondo, they continued down the hallway.

Quinn stumbled, trying to stay alongside Sarah. Absorbing all the sights, smells, and bits of conversation was hard when she had to keep dodging young folk.

Glancing at other maidens, Quinn wondered if she could pass for one of them. Her hair and pale skin made her feel as out of place as a maiden in the Hall of Knights.

She noticed other differences, too. Many of these maidens had lips the color of rubies in her father's crown, rosy cheeks, and dark eyes with shaded lids.

"Sarah?" Quinn grabbed her sleeve to slow her down. "Why do maidens wear colors on their faces?"

Sarah stopped and studied Quinn's face. "That's it!" she exclaimed. "That's what's missing. Come on." She took Quinn's elbow and steered her sideways through the crowd, then into a room marked GIRLS.

Inside, a row of doors covered one wall; a row of washbasins ran along the other.

Above the basins were looking glasses. A dozen maidens vied for a spot in front of each glass, combing their hair and coloring their faces. The girls chittered to each other, making Quinn think of the sounds of the animals in the forest around the pool.

Sarah finagled a spot in front of one glass, then jerked Quinn into line. She dug into her bag, pulling out small containers. Opening them, she dabbed the contents onto the princess's face.

It tickled. Quinn had a hard time standing still, especially when Sarah combed her eyelashes with a tiny brush.

"Voilà!" Sarah spun Quinn to face her reflection.

She gawked at herself. Her lips were crimson, her cheeks blushed on their own, and her eyelids matched her green garment.

But the best part were her eyelashes. No longer pale and colorless, now they were full and long and dark — like Ameka's. She'd always envied Ameka's lashes.

Quinn wasn't sure how to react. Giggling, she said, "Now I look like a court jester."

"A court jester?" Sarah glanced at the other girls, who were watching with great curiosity. "Oh, yes, a court jester." She pretended to laugh, too.

Sarah dumped the containers into her bag, then shoved Quinn toward the door.

The princess knew everyone was staring, but she didn't care. A little outer-earth magic, and *poof!* Gone were her pale skin and lashes.

Back in the crowded hallway, Quinn thought she'd feel less conspicuous, now that she looked like an outer-earth maiden, but instead, it made her feel *more* noticeable.

Rushing along, she bowed her head to hide her face. "Where are we going now?" Quinn practically had to shout so Sarah could hear over noisy scholars.

"Homeroom," Sarah called back.

"Home? But we just got here."

Sarah gave her the look that meant she'd said something foolish. "It's the first class of the day. You'll like Mr. Muench."

A loud bell rang, making Quinn jump. This world was filled with ringing bells and buzzing buzzers.

Sarah disappeared through a portal with the numeral 31 above it.

Quinn followed, watching scholars scramble for writing tables. The chamber looked similar to the one where Cam took his lessons.

"Study time," Mr. Muench called. "Get out something to do."

Quinn took an empty table in the back, so she could observe.

Sarah took a seat in front, then passed Quinn a writing stylus and a pile of parchment. At least it looked like parchment, but was much thinner, with faint blue lines.

Suddenly a voice boomed from a small box above

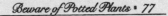

the doorway. The box trapped voices, like the telephone. This voice spoke of football games, pep rallies, and the Halloween dance.

Quinn remembered Adam's invitation to the ball. The thought of being courted by him gave her a tingly feeling, starting at the top of her head and —

Wait a minute. Quinn jerked upright in her chair. That tingly feeling only happened when —

What had she been thinking? Had she accidentally wished for something? Quinn felt sure she hadn't used the ring again by mistake.

Turning in her chair, she spotted a lone geranium in an earthen pot on the window sill.

In front of the pink flower, a wisp of a wood nymph hovered like a puff of smoke. "What's happening?" cried a tiny, tiny voice Quinn could barely hear. "Are you a witch?"

The princess felt blood drain from her face. In one instant, the entire secret of Mandria could be revealed — by a blabbering wood nymph.

"Hush!" Quinn whispered.

"Oh, this is wonderful!" the loudmouthed dryad exclaimed.

Scholars stirred, as if sensing the magic. Quinn was thankful the nymph's voice was faint. The loud voice still blasted from the box above the portal. Otherwise it would be hard to explain.

"I can talk!"

"Be quiet," Quinn hissed, glaring at the misty figure.

"Miss Mandria?" came a deep voice from the front of the room. Mr. Muench watched her over the top of his spectacles.

He glanced at a scroll in his hand as he moved to to get a better look at his newest student. "Miss Quinn Mandria is it? Please find something to do or I will give you an assignment."

"Yes, sire."

Scholars around her snickered.

Embarrassed, Quinn bent over the parchment, contemplating what to write. All morning she'd had an overwhelming urge to record all that was happening to her on outer earth. Now was her chance.

She searched the desk for an inkwell, but couldn't find one. Then she realized the ink came from inside the stylus Sarah had given her.

She smiled to herself. _Magic._

Quinn tried to ignore the indecipherable mumblings coming from the wood nymph, and concentrate on her writing.

All of a sudden the voice from the box stopped.

Quiet filled the room. Quiet, except for the geranium's gibberish. Scholars began to glance around the room, looking for the source of the voice.

"That's enough!" Quinn whispered, louder than she'd meant to.

"Miss Mandria, do I have to ask you a second time?" The schoolmaster rose from his desk, cocking an ear in her direction. "Do you have a radio?"

The nymph had burst into song.

The princess grabbed her parchment and fled to an empty table as far from the flower as she could get.

Quinn caught Sarah's disapproving frown. _She thinks I'm drawing attention to myself on purpose. Nothing could be further from the truth._

She ducked her head, but felt everyone's eyes on her. How could she convince outer-earth folk she was exactly like them if she couldn't get away from the magic?

Mr. Muench's shadow fell across her table. "I don't know what school you've come from, young lady, but we have rules here that are meant to be followed. If you've got a radio, I suggest you leave it in your locker or it will be confiscated."

Quinn glanced sideways at Sarah, who was now watching her with sympathetic eyes. She'd have to ask the maiden what a radio was.

Sarah touched two fingers to her cheek, forming

the sign of the Lorik, as if reminding Quinn of the great secret they shared.

Quinn waited until Mr. Muench moved away, then nodded at Sarah, returning the Lorik sign.

Of course I will keep the secret of Mandria, she vowed. *I must keep it.*

10

Blending In

After homeroom, the rest of the morning ran smoothly. No one singled her out again.

Quinn made a point not to speak to anyone — or sit near any plants.

World history was an interesting class, since she knew so little about outer earth. The schoolmaster gave a lecture about third-world countries. Quinn wondered where the first and second worlds were.

She scribbled plenty of notes. Would this be news to Melikar? Or was he knowledgeable about all three worlds?

In English lit, she read a story from a book called *Knights of the Round Table*. Quinn was thrilled to find the book full of stories about her great-great — however many it was — grandfather, King Arthur. She'd heard the sad love story of Arthur and Queen Guinevere many times, and it always made her misty.

Her family's link to people in this world made them *almost* like outer-earth folk. The magic touching their lives for generations had transformed them into a race that was similar, yet more in touch with all things supernatural.

Quinn began to feel pleased about her earthly adventure. Melikar had nothing to worry about. She hadn't given away any secrets. And — except for an occasional bout of homesickness and her annoyance with Zack — she seemed to be fitting into this world quite well.

The last lesson before noon feast was algebra. At first Quinn wasn't sure what algebra was. A quick glance at the textbook told her it was only numerals. She was good at numerals. But when the schoolmistress put formulas and equations on the board, Quinn became confused.

Then she remembered the time Melikar showed her his potions in written form. They were so similar to these formulas, thinking of them as potions made the equations easier to solve.

The *problem* with algebra was that Zack was in the class.

He watched her with narrowed eyes, making her feel as out of place as a Marnie in a faery's hamlet.

She thought about wishing him into the next kingdom, then realized she didn't know if there *were* other kingdoms on outer earth.

After class, Sarah asked her to wait in the hall while she spoke to the mistress about her grades.

As Quinn stepped through the portal, Zack bumped her, spilling books from her hands. She sensed he'd done it on purpose.

Quinn knelt to gather her books, hoping Zack would be gone when she stood.

He wasn't.

"Hey, little cousin," he said. "You're going to the dance with me Friday night." Not waiting for an answer, he turned abruptly and strode away.

The familiar cold feeling chilled Quinn once more. "I can't," she called to his retreating form.

"You will," he threw back over his shoulder.

"No!" She ran after him, balancing the armload of books she'd collected during each class. "I already have an escort."

Zack stopped and faced her. "You already have an *escort?*" he repeated, mimicking her. "Who? Or should I say, *whom?*"

The hallway filled with other scholars. "Adam."

"Adam? You're going on a date with a *relative?*"

"Oh, he's not . . . well . . ." Quinn remembered the story Sarah had told everyone. Was being escorted by a relative an outer-earth taboo? In Mandria, it was common.

She didn't know what to say. Why was Zack taunting her like this? Quinn's eyes firmly met his. "I'm *not* going to the ball with you." She turned to hurry away, and immediately bumped into Sarah.

"There you are." Sarah's gaze traveled beyond her to Zack's retreating form. The maiden's pleasantness disappeared. "What did he want?"

Was Sarah unhappy about the attention Zack was giving her? Well, so was she.

"He didn't want anything." The princess sighed. "He was just . . . talking." How could Sarah be fond of a knave who acted like he did?

Sarah acted as if it didn't matter, then led Quinn to a gigantic chamber marked CAFETERIA.

The aroma of hot food reminded Quinn she was hungry. She wasn't used to being hungry. A mere snap of her fingers in Mandria brought any delicacy she desired.

"Follow me," Sarah called above the sounds of clinking utensils and loud voices. "And do what I do." She stopped at the end of a line of scholars.

Quinn joined the line, watching Sarah select dishes of food, putting them onto a tray. Quinn did the same, craning her neck to see what smelled so delicious. The spicy aroma reminded her of Melikar's chamber.

Absorbed by the process of the orderly line, Quinn kept one eye on the round dish with the intriguing smell. A servant cut the food into slices, then set out the trays so young folk could help themselves.

"What is that?" Quinn whispered, pointing.

"Pizza," Sarah whispered back.

Quinn had never seen anything like it. She _had_ to taste it. The aroma alone was making her mouth water.

She watched those ahead choose the dish until there were only a few slices left. It was almost her turn. _Hurry_, she thought as she watched the slices disappear. Sarah would get the last piece.

Bats, Quinn swore, borrowing Cam's favorite curse. Her eyes scanned the area. No one was watching; there was too much commotion in the room. Sarah scooped the last piece onto her plate, and moved on down the line.

Quinn twisted the magic ring, and wished for one more slice.

Her hand was there to grab it the moment it appeared.

Warmth flushed her cheeks until the tingling sensation subsided.

No one said a word. She'd done it! Pleasure made her smile as she licked spicy sauce from her fingers.

Quinn's feeling of pleasure was short-lived as an

image of the wizard rose in her mind. What had possessed her to use the magic for something so trivial?

A vague premonition of danger crept over her. How foolish of her to ignore Melikar's warning. She vowed never to do it again.

Sarah was bartering for her lunch with a large matron, who pushed buttons on top of a slanted box, making it beep. Quinn nudged Sarah. "I have nothing with which to barter."

"It's okay." Sarah handed bills and coins to the matron. "Mondo gave me lunch money for both of us."

Quinn recognized the coins. She'd seen similar ones scattered across the floor of Melikar's chamber.

As she picked up her lunch tray and stepped from the line, Quinn bumped into someone. Even before turning, the smell of spirits told her it was Zack.

Quinn shivered in spite of the overheated room. How long had Zack been standing there? Had he seen her use the magic?

"There's something weird about you," he whisper-growled, refusing to let her pass. "But I'll figure it out."

The lad faked a smile so others would think they were merely chatting. "Meanwhile," he added, "I'll be watching. . . ."

11

Unwanted Attention

Quinn sat on a long bench, stair-stepping down to a grassy field stretching out below. A group of lads, including Zack, raced from one end of the field to the other, chasing after a funny-shaped ball.

"Hey!" called a voice.

The princess lifted a hand to shield her eyes from the sun.

Adam sprinted up the benches and sat beside her. "What are you doing out here by yourself?"

"Waiting for Sarah." Quinn gestured toward the side of the field where Sarah chatted with other maidens and a lad with red hair. "She didn't want to lose me, so she brought me along, then made me stay up here while she talked to her friends."

Quinn knew she didn't have to mention the

obvious — Sarah wanted to get rid of her "royal shadow," but couldn't.

"Sarah didn't come out here to talk to her friends. She came to watch Zack." Adam pronounced the lad's name as though it were a curse.

Quinn silently agreed with his reaction.

"He's a jock," Adam said. "He's decent when he hasn't been drinking, but once he starts, his personality changes. Sarah's made a fool of herself over him for months — lightening her hair because he likes blondes; trying out for cheerleader because he likes the popular girls."

Although Quinn didn't know what a _cheerleader_ was, she felt moved by Adam's protectiveness of his sister. It reminded her of the way Cam fussed whenever they ventured outside the castle on one of their jaunts.

Of course Cam's "concern" may have been nothing more than Melikar's life-or-death warning that her safety was his sole responsibility.

Adam pulled a cap from his knapsack to shade his face. "Sometimes I think my sister sent her good sense on a permanent vacation."

He glanced at Quinn. "I don't like the way Zack's tailing you. It was dumb of me to think he wouldn't notice you right off."

Quinn brushed windblown hair from her face. "What makes you think he's following me?"

"I *know* he is — because I am, too." Adam gave her a sheepish grin. "But *I* just want to make sure you're all right."

Shoving his hands into the pockets of his jacket, he scooted close, nudging Quinn with one shoulder. "You look great in my sister's clothes. And I like your hair unbraided, too."

Quinn met his gaze. Relaxing with Adam meant she could let down her guard and say whatever she pleased, like she could with Cam. Sarah acted as though Quinn's "mistakes" were meant for her own personal embarrassment.

Adam reached for her hand. "I really like you." His words were soft compared to shouts coming from the field.

Quinn took a breath to calm the fluttering in her chest. *He's holding my hand!* "I like you, too," she whispered.

The noise on the field now seemed far away. The whole world consisted of only them, right here, right now.

He slipped an arm around her shoulders, pulling her close. With one finger he traced her cheek, stopping at her lips. "When did you start wearing lipstick?"

"It was your sister's idea. She — "

Before Quinn could finish, Adam kissed her,

gently, slowly, sending a rush of warmth through her, chasing away autumn's chill.

Her first kiss.

She wanted the moment to last forever — as before — but this time she was careful not to wish it away.

Adam kissed her again.

Quinn sensed a spark between them, and knew the magic ring had *nothing* to do with it.

"Heads up!" a voice shouted.

A ball came hurtling toward them.

Adam jerked away to catch it, making Quinn flinch.

Zack sprinted up the benches toward them. He wore armor on his head, and his shoulders were large and misshapen.

Adam came to his feet, flinging the ball into the burly lad's stomach.

Zack barely faltered.

He planted himself in front of them, feet spread as wide as the smirk on his face. "Hey, Dover, Coach wants to see you." He tossed the ball from one hand to the other. "Right now. Pronto. Hurry up."

"He does not." Adam faced Zack with clenched fists. "I play softball. Why would the *football* coach want to see me?" He pulled Quinn to her feet. "Come on. Let's get out of here."

Quinn hopped from one bench to the next, trying to keep her balance. She glanced back at Zack, still watching through slitted eyes as he spiraled the ball into the air.

Quickly, she looked away, angry at herself for giving him her attention. "Shouldn't we wait for Sarah?" she asked, stepping off the last bench.

The maiden was watching them with great curiosity.

Quinn waved.

Scowling, Sarah turned away.

The princess inhaled sharply, glancing at Adam to see if he'd observed Sarah's reaction.

He shrugged. "She's probably mad because Zack talked to you." His voice still sounded tight.

"But —"

"It's okay. She'll get over it."

Adam started toward the building. "We've missed the bus by now. Sarah can catch a ride with her friends." He paused. "Hey, if we hurry, we can catch a lift with Roger before he leaves the chem lab."

As they rounded a corner, a faded, blue carriage screeched to a stop beside them, honking and sputtering.

"Need a ride?" a voice called.

"Come on." Adam stepped into the avenue and opened the back door so Quinn could climb inside.

"Hi," the lad said, grinning at her. "Welcome to Roger's taxi service."

Quinn stared at him. His eyes and skin were as golden brown as a Glaston from the kingdom of Glastonbury. She'd noticed other scholars with varying shades of skin color, and wondered about the connection between races above and below the earth.

Adam climbed into the front seat.

With a lurch and a jerk, they were off, careening down the avenue.

Quinn studied the inside of the carriage, decorated with stickers, signs, and pictures — mostly of pretty girls. It was quite different from Mondo's carriage.

During the ride home, Roger and Adam talked and teased, switching topics so rapidly that Quinn felt more confused than informed.

Trying to interpret their conversation was a strain. Giving up, she watched, captivated, as Roger steered — moving levers, pushing buttons, yelling at other drivers, and singing along with music coming from somewhere in front of them.

"I truly like your carriage," she told him during a lull in conversation.

Roger turned, shooting her a puzzled look.

Adam groaned. Leaning over the seat, he whispered close to her ear. "It's a _car_."

Quinn melted into the seat as Roger attempted to stare at her and keep his eyes on the avenue at the same time.

She bit her lip.

How am I supposed to pick my words carefully? I never know if I've said something wrong until it's too late. . . .

12

Unanswered Questions

When they arrived at the apartment, Adam retreated to his sleeping chamber to do his lessons.

Quinn wandered into Sarah's chamber and curled up on the bed. She wanted to record the events of the past two days in a journal she'd created with parchment and a binder Adam had lent her.

Sarah arrived, quickly gathered a few things, and headed to another room in the apartment.

Why was she being unfriendly? Because of Zack?

When Quinn finished noting her thoughts, she wandered into the cooking chamber to watch Mondo and Sarah prepare the evening feast.

The maiden placed eating vessels on the table, then pushed buttons on a machine to chop an onion. Quinn thought it a complicated way to chop vegetables.

Next Sarah placed a plate in a shiny box with buttons. The food heated in seconds — without fire! Quinn's amazement was unending.

The feast consisted of chopped greens, meat, and cheese, scooped into a stiff, tan shell. Food on outer earth was unique. Quinn hoped she'd remember to mention it in her journal.

In Mandria, she ate a lot of porridge, soups, and stews. Vegetables came from the food-growing chambers, and meat from the herds maintained by Marnies.

During dinner, conversation between her and Sarah was strained. It worried Quinn. Maybe later, she could speak to the maiden alone.

After the repast, Adam and Sarah disappeared into another chamber.

Quinn helped Mondo put things away, grateful for the opportunity to ask a few of the multitude of questions jumbling through her mind.

"Sire," she began in a hushed voice, wanting to come right to the point. "How do you know of the sign of the Lorik?"

Mondo carried the last vessels from the table to the scullery. He was quiet so long, Quinn wasn't sure he'd heard her question. "Mondo?"

He raised a hand to silence her, then held her attention with his pool-colored eyes. "Sometimes it's better not to know too much. This is one of those times." He calmly began to gather empty goblets from the table.

Her face burned. He was her only connection to Mandria; he *couldn't* shut her out. "*Tell* me."

"Quinn." Mondo's voice was sharp. His expression told her that *he* knew *she* knew the Mandrian truth she was about to break: *When an elder dismisses a youth, the youth is bound to obey.*

She bowed her head in compliance.

"Now." Mondo tossed a linen over one shoulder, continuing in a lighter tone. "Go into the living room. There's something in there you might find interesting."

Disappointed, Quinn wandered into the living chamber. Adam and Sarah were sprawled on the cushions, staring at a large box on a stand.

Pictures flashed inside the box. People with terror-streaked faces were fleeing in alarm as fiery explosions burst around them.

Quinn sank to her knees in front of the box, covering her face with her hands. "What is it?"

"The evening news." Adam didn't seem bothered at all. With a flick of a wand, he made the sound stop. "They're showing clips of a war taking place on the other side of the world."

"Oh, it's terrible," Quinn whispered.

The screen now showed children running, laughing, and tumbling over each other, a lot like children in Mandria.

She watched, hypnotized by images flashing onto the screen.

Mondo joined them. For a moment, a cozy feeling warmed Quinn. Her family and guests always gathered in front of the giant hearth in their living chamber after the evening feast.

Adam touched her shoulder. "Let's go for a walk. You can wear one of my jackets."

Surprised and pleased by the invitation, she followed him to the portal.

As he bundled her into an oversized coat with a large letter C on the front, Quinn felt Mondo's eyes studying them.

A quick glance at his face told her he disapproved of the two of them leaving together.

"Don't be gone long," he said in a brusque tone.

Why would he disapprove? Was he trying to protect her? Or Adam? He might be wiser to disapprove of Sarah's foolishness over Zack.

Puzzled by Mondo's gruffness, Quinn dared a final glance as Adam opened the portal.

Mondo's look of disapproval had turned to one of deep, deep sorrow.

13

A Future Set in Stone

Quinn wrapped Adam's jacket around her shoulders, blocking the chilled night air.

The change of seasons wasn't as noticeable under the river as it was here. Only in the upper parts of the kingdom could one feel the cold hardness of earth during fall and winter, and the moist warmness in spring and summer.

Adam kept his arm tight around Quinn as he steered her at a brisk pace. The urgency in his actions puzzled her.

Finally they stopped to sit on a low fence surrounding a park, dimly lit by lamp posts. Adam sat in silence for a long moment, then faced her, swinging one leg over the fence as though he were straddling a horse.

"Princess," he whispered, taking hold of her hands. "How long are you going to stay with us?"

The question caught her by surprise. Things had happened so fast since she'd found herself sitting on top of the footbridge, she hadn't had time to consider which she desired most — staying or leaving.

Nor had she thought of the *mission* with which she'd tried to influence Melikar. The idea of traveling here with a "message" now seemed foolish. Outer-earth folk had more to teach *her*, than she *them*.

Adam's scrutiny was causing her great discomfort. Never had she worried over how she appeared. Her proper attire for each royal occasion was based on what had been worn for centuries, selected by her ladies — or by Jalla, her old nanny, who made sure the princess's ladies did what they were supposed to.

Now she found herself longing to be prettier, to own stylish clothes, to cut her hair. Her mind's eye immediately formed the image of an appalled and irate Melikar.

Adam nudged her. "Are you going to answer me?"

Quinn sighed. "I don't know how long I'm staying."

The wind tousled hair across her face. Adam brushed it back so tenderly, his simple gesture almost broke her heart.

"I don't feel at home here," she told him. "I miss my parents and Ameka. And even Cam and Scrabit, and — "

"Scrabit?"

"My pet dragon."

Adam's jaw dropped. "You have a pet *dragon?*"

"Yes. A small one. He's a little bigger than Katze will be when he's grown."

Adam shook his head. "If I hadn't seen the magic with my own eyes, I would never believe I was sitting here with a princess who owned a magic ring and a pet dragon."

"I guess it seems a bit odd to you."

"*Odd* isn't even close." He lifted her hands to his lips and kissed them. "I want you to stay with us for as long as you can. You are . . . um . . ." He faltered, watching her face as though he were memorizing it. "You're beautiful," he finished in a whisper.

Quinn shivered at his gentle words.

In spite of Adam's presence — and his compliments — talking of Mandria made the princess feel terribly melancholy.

Why was she considering choices at all? Her future didn't *offer* choices. She *must* return home — and soon — before the king did something drastic, like throw Melikar and Cam into the dungeon.

Her predicament wasn't *their* fault. *She* was the one who'd wanted to come to this world. Yet how much lighter her burden would be if she could choose the time and place of her return.

Then there was Adam.

The first lad to stir her heart. The first lad to kiss her.

How could she bid him good-bye when there was so much more she wanted to know about him?

Quinn shifted sideways and put her arms around his neck. "I cannot stay long in your world. I don't know what will happen to me here."

"*Nobody* knows what will happen to them."

"That's not true. I know *exactly* what my life will be like — in Mandria."

"How could you possibly know?"

"It's a Mandrian truth. I'm a princess and an only child. My sixteenth birthday will begin with an official coming-of-age ceremony."

"What does that mean?"

"It's an open invitation for all young lads of noble blood, from the farthest corners of all the underground kingdoms, to come courting."

Sadness touched Adam's face. "I'm afraid to ask, but what happens next?"

"From all who come, I must choose. A nobleman

who meets my father's approval, of course. The castle will immediately prepare for my wedding celebration, which will fall a quarter moon after my birthday.

"The king proclaims a holiday, lasting for three days. Then, after a wedding trip, I will be expected to bear many grandchildren for my father, especially a son who will become king when I die."

"Who will be king when your father dies?"

"Me. I mean, I'll be queen since there are no male heirs."

"Wow." Adam whistled under his breath. "Amazing."

He cocked his head. "What if none of the young suitors with noble blood appeals to you?"

Quinn loved the way he was gazing at her. She sensed his jealousy, and it made her like him all the more.

Afraid to read what his eyes were telling her, she looked away. "If I don't decide in a proper amount of time, the choice will be made for me."

"By the king?"

She nodded.

"Is that what you want?" His words turned harsh. "A blueprinted life with no surprises or unexpected twists?"

Quinn didn't know what "blueprinted" meant, but

she'd learned long ago not to question her predictable future. "That's the way it is, Adam. It's a — "

"Mandrian truth," he finished, now sounding bitter. "The princess marries a nobleman and they live happily ever under." He gave a weak laugh at his own cleverness.

Adam tried to pull away, but Quinn kept her arms tight around his neck. "There's no sense upsetting yourself about it."

"Why not?"

"Because I don't know _how_ to return to Mandria."

"You don't?"

She thought he sounded pleased. "All I can do is guess."

Adam leaned his forehead against hers. "Then let's not consider your leaving an option."

"But, I might be _forced_ to leave."

"Why?"

She hushed her voice. "I sense danger here."

"Danger?" He drew back. "What? Who? Are you in danger?"

"Maybe _I'm_ not, but the whole secret of my kingdom's existence is in danger simply by my being here. If the wrong person finds out — " She paused, watching his face.

Adam clutched her to him. "I don't want to think

about you leaving." His voice trembled. "Everyone I care about leaves."

Quinn knew he was thinking of his parents. She held onto him, as if letting go would break the magic spell they'd woven.

Squeezing her eyes shut, she begged the confusion of her predicament to leave her alone.

No matter how hard she tried to squelch the truth, her deepest heart told her she'd already chosen the young man who caught her fancy.

And the choice frightened the princess so much, she wouldn't allow herself to ponder it.

14

For Lack of a Spell . . .

In the darkness of early morning, a ringing alarm exploded in the middle of Quinn's dream.

Sarah was not there to silence the bothersome noise.

Quinn rose from bed and snatched the offending box off a shelf. She shook it, but the ringing didn't stop.

Katze, snoozing on the window sill, was no help at all.

Quinn twisted a knob. The ringing stopped and music began to play.

Music was fine. Much less annoying than a buzzer.

Returning to bed, she curled up again, trying to recall the warm dream from which she'd been rudely yanked.

As she willed her mind back inside the mist of her dream, a feeling of shame flooded her senses.

She had been kissing someone!

Adam, of course.

No. It was Cam. She had been kissing Cam!

Quinn pulled herself up with an abruptness that startled Katze. Why would she dream such a thing? She missed him; he was her friend. Yet in her dream, she'd been kissing Cam the way Adam had kissed her.

The princess's skin grew warm. She touched her face. It felt tender and sore. Getting out of bed, she stumbled to the looking glass above the cabinet. Her face was red. How could it be? Could a shameful dream leave one with a blush that refused to fade?

Worried, Quinn slipped into one of Sarah's robes and rushed to find her.

She found Adam instead.

"Wow." He lifted her chin. "You got sunburned yesterday at the football field."

"Sunburned?" Quinn echoed, relieved to know she wasn't being permanently punished for her shame.

"I should've known your skin would burn easily." He looked apologetic. "Guess I'm not taking good care of you, like I promised."

Opening a hall cabinet, Adam rummaged through it. "Here's something to make your skin feel better." He handed her a bottle, then continued down the hall to get ready for school.

Quinn decided to fetch a goblet of juice before dressing. In the cooking chamber, she found Sarah, already dressed, and Mondo. Both were at the table, studying large pieces of parchment. They mumbled, "Good morning," but nothing more.

Katze, who'd followed the princess, was the only friendly one. He nudged her leg, purring. She helped herself to a muffin and juice, carrying her morning feast back to Sarah's chamber.

After showering, Quinn dabbed on the ointment Adam had given her. What about garments for today? Helping herself to Sarah's clothes without asking would only anger the maiden more.

Quinn dressed in the same garments she'd worn the day before. Gathering her binder and stylus, she went outside to wait on the front steps for the bus.

She was beginning to feel as out of place as she did during visits to the candle chamber. Hardworking Marnies scurried here and there. She never knew where to stand, or if it was all right to sit at a workbench.

And she never knew whether to ask questions or

keep silent, if it was all right to play with the Marnies' cats — of which they were very possessive — or simply ignore the cats' antics.

Quinn thought it odd to be having the same feelings in this world. She could *not* stay if she were causing problems. Should she find somewhere else to lodge? Or was this a sign to go home?

Holding out her hand, she studied Cam's ring. Maybe all she had to do was wish upon the ring. Why hadn't she thought of it before?

Shoving the binder off her lap, she twisted the ring once.

Wait.

Was she truly ready to leave? Shouldn't she say good-bye first?

Why? her mind argued. *Sarah wants you gone, and Mondo acts as though he does, too.*

She gave the ring a second twist.

Adam didn't want her to leave; she felt sure of that. But wouldn't he be better off if she left now instead of later? Before their feelings for each other deepened? He'd understand if she didn't say good-bye. Wouldn't he?

Taking a deep breath, Quinn twisted the ring a third time.

Closing her eyes, she imagined Mandria: turrets topping the castle walls; the coziness of her sleeping chamber; colorful tapestries covering cold, stone walls.

A tingle shivered through her. She breathed in, smelling the damp earthiness of home.

She heard Marnies galloping along the tunnels.

She saw Melikar gazing into the fire on his hearth.

She pictured herself stepping along the avenues, wearing her outer-earth garments, hair flowing free, eyelashes dark and curled.

Mandrians stopped to point at her, and —

"Are you okay?"

Cam! Her heart surged with joy as she opened her eyes.

Adam bent over her.

"Let's go," he said. "The bus is waiting."

Quinn's joy traded places with relief. As much as she wanted to go home, part of her couldn't resist staying here to find out *what might happen next.*

It was like living one of the storybooks Ameka chose for her to read.

The tingling sensation was gone now. Quinn gathered her things, stepping aside on the stairs as Sarah bounded past.

Boarding the bus with the other passengers reminded her of the shuttle at Wonderland Park. How quickly she had learned the proper way to act.

The seats were almost full, preventing her and

Adam from sitting together. Sarah sat next to a red-haired lad named Scott. Quinn chose a seat next to a maiden who was reading — so she wouldn't have to talk.

She wanted to ponder why Cam's ring hadn't worked.

Why were accidental wishes granted, but true wishes were not?

Had she not wished correctly? Or was it fate?

Yet fate could be altered by magic, and magic *had* been sparked by her wish; she'd felt it. Maybe the ring's power was willing, but lacked a spell to move her between the two worlds.

The theory made Quinn's heart sag. In the back of her mind, she'd trusted the ring to take her home the instant she was ready. If a spell was necessary, she had bigger troubles than she'd imagined.

How could she conjure a spell? She wasn't an enchantress.

She thought of Cam's words:

> *Anger, fear, love, and mirth.*
> *Send Quinn and Cam to outer earth.*

Funny. She'd experienced every one of those emotions since arriving here.

Quinn rested her head against the seat. "Is it true, Melikar?" she whispered. "Can I *not* come home by my own accord?"

She closed her eyes against tears that threatened to spill down her cheeks. *What have I done? Will I never see my kingdom again?*

15

Testing the Magic

The school day was uneventful. Teachers didn't call on Quinn to answer questions — maybe because she was new. Yet a heaviness followed her everywhere.

Three worries troubled her heart:

One. The ring's magic did not take her home.

Two. Sarah's heart was closed to her.

Three. Zack.

Yesterday, Quinn had relied so much on Sarah's help. Now she was having difficulty finding classrooms. And it seemed like everywhere she turned, Zack was there, watching.

Coming to school today had been foolish. Her patience was being stretched to its limit.

So. She'd had her taste of outer-earth lessons. It was time to return to the apartment and stay — only she didn't know how to get there.

The act of making plans was such a novelty, Quinn almost felt giddy. Plans were always made _for_ her. No one ever asked what _she_ felt like doing.

Well, now the princess would do what _she_ desired. It was settled. No more lessons.

At lunchtime, Quinn slipped outside to be alone. She didn't have coins to barter for food, since Mondo had given her share to Sarah.

A misty rain began to fall. Quinn stepped under the branches of a tree for shelter. Leaning against the trunk, she breathed in the fresh scent of falling rain, feeling truly alone for the first time in her life.

In some ways, being alone was a luxury, yet she wouldn't wish for long spells of it.

Shivering, she hugged herself. The branches of the tree bent close, blocking the chilly wind.

"Thank you," she mumbled, accepting the fact that the tree was sheltering her.

She knew it was the tree's wood nymph, awakened by the surrounding magic, yet she smiled to think how startled an observant passerby might be.

The wood nymph didn't answer. Quinn searched the base of the trunk, but did not see a maiden's smoky form. Was the aura of magic fading?

She wondered if the _ring's_ magic would remain strong. Should she test it? For what could she wish that wasn't frivolous?

Ah, food. She was terribly hungry. Surely Melikar wouldn't begrudge her something to eat.

Twisting the ring, Quinn wished for a piece of fruit.

The familiar tingling shivered through her. A rustling of red and gold leaves drew her attention. In a heartbeat, the branches above her burst with plump, juicy apples.

She plucked two, one for now, one for later, feeling thankful the power in the ring remained strong.

At the end of the day, Adam found the princess and escorted her to the large room where her last class met to exercise and play sports. The floor was covered with mats on which lads were wrestling.

Quinn and Adam sat on a bench to watch Roger and a boy from another village compete.

Adam started to explain the sport to Quinn, but she recognized it as one that was popular with knights and peasants alike in Mandria.

Zack was there, too. He won every match, always looking to see if Quinn was watching. She tried to ignore him, but he put on such a display, it was hard not to notice.

The minute Adam left to get a drink, Zack approached, blocking her view of the wrestlers.

"Still dating your cousin?" he quipped, watching her face for a reaction.

She didn't give him one.

"Everybody knows you two aren't cousins," he added. "What we *don't* know is why you told everyone you were. Why *did* you?"

Quinn disregarded him, scooting over on the bench until she could see the wrestlers again.

"Well, if you won't answer that, answer this: Have you pulled any rabbits out of a hat today?"

She'd have to ask Adam what that meant.

Zack leaned a brawny arm on the bench next to her. "Tell me how you did that trick," he demanded. "The one in the lunch line. And how you shocked me on the bus."

Quinn kept her eyes on the wrestling match, trying not to react.

"Are you magic?" he added, chuckling.

Her eyes darted to his. Did he know? Or was he guessing?

Adam returned with Roger, who'd finished his match. "What do *you* want?" he muttered to the intruder.

Zack straightened, emphasizing his tallness. He put both hands behind his head and flexed his muscles. "Since there's a misunderstanding about who's taking Quinn to the dance," he said with a sneer, "why don't you and I wrestle tomorrow after school? The winner will take her."

Quinn started to protest, then stopped, not sure if it was acceptable for a maiden to interfere when one lad challenged another.

Adam and Zack glared at each other.

Roger placed a hand on Adam's shoulder. "Not fair, Zack. Adam isn't on the wrestling team. If you're going to challenge him, make it something neutral."

Quinn glanced from one lad to the other. Their eyes stayed locked in an angry staring match. Her heart pounded in resentment at Zack's unwanted intrusion into her life.

"Fists," Adam suggested calmly.

Zack grinned.

"No!" Quinn interrupted, not caring if it were proper or not. With mental apologies to Adam, she could plainly see Zack was much stronger.

"What then, little cousin?" Zack asked. "A duel?"

"No!" she cried again, not knowing whether or not he was serious.

She blurted the first thing that came to mind. "A jousting match."

All three lads stared at her.

"In the alley behind the school," she added. "If I

must attend the ball with the winner, then I agree to do so."

Zack looked confused, then lowered his arms, acting indifferent. "I'll be there." He bounded off the benches and stormed away.

Quinn smiled in triumph.

Roger raised an eyebrow, giving her a puzzled look. "Excuse me? Would you care to explain jousting match?"

Adam groaned. "I, too, would like to know the cause of my future death."

Quinn ignored their teasing. "A jousting match," she told them, "is what everyone suggests when they're challenged."

"Everyone who?" Roger asked.

Was this Mandrian ritual unknown in the outer world? "Two lads face each other on horseback," she explained. "Then they charge. Each tries to knock the other off his horse with a lance."

"I was _hoping_ that wasn't the kind of jousting you meant." Adam acted as if she'd embarrassed him. "Horses are a little hard to come by in the 'burbs, and — "

"Wait," Roger interrupted. "I've got a great idea. Let's go."

After changing clothes, he drove them to his house.

Once there, Roger rounded up a coil of rope and two oars from his father's canoe. They helped him pad the oars with pillows, then Roger jabbed Adam a few times, trying out the "lances."

"They work, they work." Adam grimaced, holding his stomach. "Now, where are we going to find horses?"

"Wait here." Roger disappeared, then returned with two boards on wheels. "Skateboards," he proclaimed. "Twentieth-century horses."

The lads squared off in the alley behind Roger's house.

Quinn clapped her hands to start the match. They charged, flying past her on the skateboards. She hopped to one side as they swished past, barely missing her. Both were hesitant to use lances on each other.

Quinn sat on the ground to watch the competition. The sight of two lads performing an outer-earth version of an ancient Mandrian tradition thrilled her — even though these lads tumbled a lot.

After a while, they improved enough to stay on the boards longer. Sore and tired, they made plans to practice once more before the match, then Roger drove them home, promising he'd fill Zack in on the details of the new "sport" they'd invented.

In spite of Quinn's worry over Adam's challenge,

she was secretly pleased to know *she* was the prize for which they jousted.

Such was an honor for any Mandrian maiden.

When they arrived home, Mondo had already left for work, and Sarah was in her sleeping chamber. The evening feast still simmered on the cookstove. Quinn was famished after eating only apples for lunch.

After the meal, she took her time cleaning the scullery — partly because she'd never done it before, and partly to put off confronting Sarah. When finished, Quinn took a deep breath, and headed down the hallway to Sarah's chamber.

On the floor outside the portal, lay her royal gown in a crumpled heap.

Dismayed, Quinn tapped on the door, gathering her dress and shaking out the wrinkles.

Sarah didn't respond, so Quinn opened the door with a hesitant hand.

The maiden was working at her writing table.

"May I come in?"

"No," Sarah mumbled, not lifting her head.

Quinn entered anyway and closed the door. "Why are you so angry with me?"

Sarah scrunched her face, as if she couldn't believe Quinn had asked such a foolish question. "Why am

I angry? You've moved into my room uninvited, helped yourself to my clothes, helped yourself to my boyfriend — "

"Oh, bother," Quinn interrupted. "First of all, I thought you *wanted* me to stay. You offered your clothes — "

"Mondo offered my clothes."

Quinn paused. She couldn't argue; Sarah was right. "And if *boyfriend* refers to Zack," she added, "I can explain."

"Oh, *sure* you can. You've been flirting with him ever since you got here. Now if he talks to me at all, it's only to ask me about you." She looked as if she were about to cry.

"I did nothing to encourage — "

"You didn't *have* to do anything! He likes you anyway."

Sarah flung a stylus across the room. "Why don't you go back where you came from?" Stomping to the door, she yanked it open. "You're not sleeping in my room anymore. And I want my clothes back, too."

Quinn fled from the chamber, feeling as if she'd been slapped across the face. In this world, being a princess meant absolutely nothing.

She found Adam in front of the picture box. Still

clutching her gown, she slumped beside him on the cushions and told him what happened.

Adam simply laughed. "To my sister, everything is a tragedy." He pushed a button on the small wand in his hand, making the images on the screen change. "Zack's not her boyfriend; she only *thinks* he is. As a matter of fact, Scott, the guy with red hair, is crazy about her. Only she doesn't even notice."

"What should I do?" Quinn heard her voice quiver. "I can't wear my gown in public, and now I have no place to sleep."

"Yes, you do." Adam pushed another button, causing the screen to grow dark. "You'll sleep in my room, and I'll kick Katze off the couch and sleep here."

He took the gown from her and hung it in a wardrobe. "I guess now's as good a time as any to take you shopping. Mondo asked why you were wearing the same clothes you wore yesterday, so I filled him in on the way Sarah's been resenting you. He gave me money to buy whatever you want."

Adam fetched a cloak for her, and they walked down the avenue to a row of shops. Quinn had never seen so many items for barter in all her life.

In Mandria, there were three types of gowns: formal for balls or cultural events; dressy for pageants or afternoon teas; and simple for morning lessons.

Here, dozens of shops overflowed with multiple garments for the choosing. With Adam's guidance, she selected a variety, plus shoes, and even her own pots of color for her face!

On the way home, Quinn kept peeking at her earthly purchases with delight. Yet she had a niggling notion that Melikar would *not* approve.

Sighing, she pondered why the invisible wizard held so much power over her thoughts and feelings.

She could almost hear his gravelly voice chiding her: "*Mandrian blood flows through your veins, yet the trappings of outer earth are drawing you as powerfully as a moth is drawn to a candle's flame. . . .*"

16

Foiled Plans

Quinn felt guilty taking over Adam's sleeping chamber, but he assured her he'd be fine on the sofa, as he'd called it.

After laying out her new clothes, she undressed, pulling an old blue shirt of Adam's over her head. The shirt was the only thing she could find in his closet to sleep in.

She hugged it. Having something of Adam's around her made her feel safe.

Taking a tour of his chamber, she studied his possessions: a trophy engraved with his name; the cap he always wore; and a picture of a smiling, waving man and woman. The family resemblance told her it was Adam's father and mother.

Quinn tried to imagine losing her own parents, and

hoped the time was long in coming. She admired Adam and Sarah for going on with their lives so bravely, without a mother and father to console their sadnesses and cheer their successes.

Homesickness consumed her. Two days had passed, yet somehow it seemed much longer.

Yawning, she glanced about the chamber for a candle to snuff. Remembering where she was, the princess overlooked her temporary forgetfulness and clicked off the light.

Curling up in Adam's bed was so comforting, Quinn soon fell asleep, peaceful for the first time since arriving in this world.

The pleasantness was still with her in the fog of wakening, but instantly vanished when she recalled what the day would bring: The joust.

A premonition of danger had troubled her dreams throughout the night. Under the river, premonitions were taken seriously, and Quinn's were usually as accurate as a Marnie's.

She must warn Adam of her foreboding dream about the unevenly matched joust.

She didn't trust Zack. And she'd never forgive herself if Adam was injured because of her.

Zack was a bully. There were bullies in Mandria, too. Adam did *not* have to prove himself to her — or anyone.

Rising, she padded into the living chamber. Adam was gone.

Then she remembered. He'd planned to leave early this morning so he and Roger could practice jousting one last time.

Bats, Quinn cursed. This meant she'd have to go to school after all. She'd planned to stay here, spending the day writing in her journal and exploring the avenues around the apartment.

Finding Adam is more urgent, her mind told her.

Dressing in her own earthly clothes this morning was pleasurable. Tight-fitting garments and unbraided hair now felt natural. Adam had even purchased ornaments to keep her hair from falling across her face.

Quinn tried to apply the eyelash magic in the tiny looking glass over Adam's writing table, but soon realized how difficult it was. Sarah had made it look easy.

Sarah.

A heaviness settled in Quinn's chest. She missed the lightheartedness they'd shared the first day of school. Secretly, she'd hoped she and the maiden could be like sisters.

Quinn took her time getting ready. She even toyed with the idea of using the ring to whisk her to school so she wouldn't have to face Mondo and Sarah this morning.

But she knew better. Quinn *did* want to please Melikar and not worry him — especially if he were watching her with his powers.

Picking up her new jacket, she headed for the cooking chamber. Scott leaned against a cabinet, waiting to escort Sarah to school.

"Morning," Quinn said, smiling at him.

Before he could answer, Sarah grabbed his arm. "Come on, I'm ready to leave." She glowered at Quinn as they hurriedly left the apartment.

Quinn sat at the table, feeling defeated before the day had barely begun. *Did Sarah think I was being coquettish with Scott merely by saying hello?*

Frustrated, she wished she could shake some sense into the maiden. Scott and Zack were of no interest to her. All she cared about was Adam — and what was going to happen this afternoon in the alley behind the school.

Mondo appeared, carrying a roll of parchment and a cup of tea. "Good morning, dear." He gave her a cheerful smile as he took a band off the parchment and spread out the pages on the table.

Quinn attempted a smile.

Mondo filled her goblet with juice, then served pastry with bilberry jam. "I was planning to ask your opinion of this world, now that you've had a couple of days to sample it." He peered at her over the top of his spectacles. "From the look on your face, I'd guess your opinion isn't optimistic."

Quinn dipped her finger into the jam and licked it off. "Lessons are fine," she began, "quite interesting, actually — so different from my formal instruction in Mandria, but . . ." She glanced at Mondo, hesitant to complain about his own granddaughter. "I'm having difficulties with Sarah, and — "

"I know," Mondo interrupted. "Adam informed me." He took a sip of tea. "Sarah is used to being the only princess around here, if you'll pardon the expression. She's never quite recovered from the loss of her parents."

He paused, as if meditating on the thought. "Adam has handled the aftermath of the accident much better than his sister, but then, he's older. Sarah's had our love and patience, but she's never had to share us with anyone. Since you arrived, Adam has practically ignored her — not intentionally, of course, but I can tell Sarah has been unhappy these past few days."

Mondo helped himself to a pastry. "Adam will soon be leaving for college. I worry that his departure will be a great loss for his sister."

Mondo's words made Quinn feel remorseful about her impatience with Sarah. So. Zack wasn't the *only* issue that had set the maiden against her. She believed Quinn was stealing Adam away as well.

The princess sighed, promising the highest spirit she'd try again to make amends with Sarah.

Mondo adjusted his spectacles. "Other than the disharmony between you and my granddaughter, is everything else all right?"

Now was her chance to question Mondo's irregular behavior toward her. She straightened in her chair. "No. Everything else is *not* all right."

Quinn waited for him to meet her gaze. "My being here bothers you as strongly as it does Sarah. Why?"

Mondo seemed startled by her direct question. His blue-green eyes clouded as he placed a wrinkled hand on her arm. "Forgive me, child, if I've made you feel unwanted. You are *more* than welcome to share our home."

He hesitated, as if the words were painful to express. "I only wish you would not spend so much time with Adam."

"But why? Adam and I truly care for each other."

Mondo's hand jerked away. He rose with such abruptness, the juice in Quinn's goblet spilled. Swiftly he gathered the parchment from the table.

With his back to Quinn, he spoke in an emotion-choked voice, "If I could be Melikar for one brief moment, I'd cast a spell over you and Adam that was so powerful, you'd never be able to bear the sight of one another."

17

Rainbows and Deceptions

All the way to school, Mondo's words hung over Quinn's head like storm clouds. He was hiding something from her.

But what? Why was he trying so hard to keep her and Adam apart? And what was his connection to her world?

The gloomy chill made Quinn grateful for the jacket Adam had bought her. In Mandria, the air was the same every day. Here, she'd wake to warm sunshine one morning and cool cloudiness the next.

Quinn was not happy to be at school after thinking she was finished with the bother of it. But today, she was here for Adam's sake.

Between lessons, she slipped outside to the school's courtyard, anxious to be away from noisy scholars and the strain of having to watch her words and actions. Gloomy or not, she was absorbed by what Adam called *weather*.

Clouds nestled close to the earth, almost within reach. Mist moistened her cheeks, curling wisps of hair on her forehead. The heavy blanket of clouds comforted her; she'd never get used to wide-open spaces.

Hearing a tap on one of the glass-paneled walls, Quinn caught sight of Roger waving in an exagger-ated manner. She followed his slim frame with her eyes as he worked his way against the flow of young folk in the hallway and stepped outside to join her.

"Hi," he said, dropping his books onto a rock bench. "Are you crazy, coming out here in the fog?"

"Yes," she answered — to avoid a truthful expla-nation which would make him believe she *was* crazy.

Roger laughed.

"What are you going to be for Halloween?" she asked. It was a question she'd heard others asking all day.

"Didn't Adam tell you? After our jousting practice, I found a picture of two knights in armor with real lances. I showed it to my girlfriend, Wendy, and she made costumes for us.

"So, m'lady," Roger added, "we'll both be going to the dance as knights." He placed one foot in front of the other, bowing low with a flourish of his arm. "And what are *you* going to be for Halloween?"

The question caught Quinn by surprise. What sort of costume could she create? Perhaps a royal sapphire gown would do. . . .

"Mmm. Maybe I'll be a princess," she told him, trying to sound as if the idea just occurred to her — which, of course, it had.

The thought of Adam dressed as a knight gave Quinn chill bumps. She imagined him riding a white steed across the castle's drawbridge to ask the king's permission to court her.

"Hey." Roger's voice drew her back to this world. "The bell's about to ring; we'd better get inside."

A strange pain stabbed Quinn's heart as she followed Roger toward the door. Why *couldn't* Adam be one of the noble lads coming to the castle to court her when she turned sixteen?

Sighing, she glanced at the sky before stepping inside. A few clouds had parted. In between curved a hazy arch, shimmering in colorful stripes.

"Look!" Quinn cried, pointing.

Roger stopped to follow her gaze. "So?" He shrugged, holding the door for her, but she continued to stare at the sky.

Chuckling, he gave her an odd look, as if unsure

whether or not she was teasing him. "You act like you've never seen a rainbow before."

A rainbow, Quinn echoed, wishing she could stay behind to study it. *Why did Melikar tell me this world holds no magic?*

The final bell blared through Quinn's head, mercilessly reminding her of what was to happen in the alley after school.

Urgency from her premonition returned like a winter fever.

And she hadn't found Adam to tell him of it.

Some jousting matches in Mandria were fought to the death. Quinn shivered at the memory of one joust that ended in tragedy. She was young at the time, but knew the match was held to decide who would win the hand of a young maiden named Gwynnith.

During the joust, both knights lost their lives, and the maiden, in her sorrow, departed to another kingdom and never married.

Filled with foreboding thoughts, Quinn hurried from her last class — and smashed squarely into Mr. Muench.

"There you are!" he exclaimed, recovering his spectacles, which had gone flying across the hall. "I've been looking for you." He adjusted a stack of red-penciled papers.

"Go immediately to the office. They've been unable to locate your school records."

Quinn froze in her deception.

"It's quite odd actually," Mr. Muench continued. "They say the computer has no history of you whatsoever. But, computers have been known to chew up records and swallow them whole, so I'm not surprised at the mix-up. However, they do wish to speak with you, and — "

"Not now," Quinn blurted, backing away. "I have a . . . an appointment. I'll have my grandfather — I mean — " Quinn stopped, confused about what to call Mondo.

Mr. Muench shook his head. "This must be straightened out at once, Miss Mandria. You're not officially enrolled until all your records have been transferred. This is highly irregular."

Quinn gave up trying to be correct. "I'll have Mondo call the headmaster and explain."

Mr. Muench shoved on his spectacles, mumbled something about *students bending the rules at will*, then shuffled down the hallway.

Relief and annoyance filled Quinn at the same time. She'd worry later about school protocol and "missing" records. Right now she needed to fortify herself for another battle with Zack — and with Adam mixed up in it this time.

As much as she wanted to warn him, part of her sensed she was too late. How could she expect Adam to do what no young lad in Mandria would ever do? Turn his back on a challenge and walk away.

Was this Mandrian truth also an earthly truth? If so, the possible consequences made the princess shudder.

18

A Misguided Token of Luck

Quinn burst through the back door of the school. Cold air slapped her face, taking away her breath.

Dashing around a brick wall, she came to a dead stop at the sight before her. Dozens of young folk filled the alley, half surrounding Adam and Roger, and half surrounding Zack.

Word of the jousting match must have spread through the school as fast as news of which couple had begun to court and which had ended their courtship.

Quinn's gaze traveled over the crowd, searching for Sarah. The maiden wasn't there.

Of course not, Quinn told herself. How could Sarah cheer for either Adam or Zack with the princess as prize? The maiden would be wise to ignore the whole situation.

The sea of jostling bodies separating Quinn from Adam dismayed her. In Mandria, crowds parted to let the princess pass the moment she appeared.

Sighing, Quinn fought her way toward him, reaching to grab the sleeve of his jacket. "We need to talk!" she shouted over the noise.

He followed her to the back wall of the school. "What is it? Is something wrong?"

"Don't do this," she pleaded.

"Why not?" He calmly adjusted the softball catcher's chest protector he'd promised her he'd wear.

"You don't have to prove anything. Zack can't keep you from courting me. This is ridiculous."

Adam gave her a sidelong frown. "Are you implying that I'm going to lose? No way. Roger and I practiced for hours. I've gotten pretty good, and —"

Quinn clutched his arm. "It's *more* than practice." How could she say it without hurting his feelings? "Strength has a lot to do with it, and you and Zack are . . . well, mismatched."

His eyes told her she'd chosen the wrong words.

"So, you think Zack is stronger? More athletic? You think he's going to whip me?"

Adam's voice grew louder with each question. "You want me to back down like a coward? Well, thanks for the vote of confidence." He shoved his hands into heavy gloves. "If Zack's so much more of a man, then I'm sure you'll enjoy going to the dance with him."

How could he be angry? Didn't he understand the dangers of ignoring Mandrian premonitions?

Of course not.

Adam turned, edging his way through the wall of young folk.

The crowd shouted for the match to begin.

Quinn reached to stop him. "I don't *trust* Zack. He might do something underhanded to hurt you."

Adam kept walking.

Her throat burned as tears filled her eyes. She hadn't meant to wound his feelings. Why had he taken her warning the wrong way?

And why did her hunch have to be correct? A challenge *was* a challenge from one lad to another, no matter which world they lived in.

Adam's pride wouldn't allow him to turn back.

Neither would the excited crowd.

Quinn wove her way through the scholars, trying to follow him.

Roger appeared, handing Adam pads for his knees. He knelt to pull them on, allowing her a chance to catch up.

"There's one more thing," she told him.

He raised skeptical eyes to her.

Quinn whispered close to his ear. "A lady always

gives her knight a token of luck to take into a joust. It's a Mandrian truth." As she spoke, she realized she had no scarf, handkerchief, or ribbon — the usual token.

Adam rose at the urging of the crowd.

"Here," Roger said, pulling a few objects from a bag. "Don't forget your catcher's mask and batting helmet."

As he helped Adam adjust the mask, Quinn searched for something to give him. Her eyes fell upon the magic ring.

Yes! It was all she had to give. Twisting the ring off her finger, she grabbed his gloved hand. "Here, m'lord, for luck."

Adam's face twisted with further insult. "I don't need *magic* to help me win. I'd rather depend on skill."

"But it's merely a token, and — "

Adam shoved the ring at her, then grabbed the "lance" from Roger. He raised it above his head. Cheers exploded from the crowd.

"And *what*?" he added. "Zack might kill me? Is that what you were going to say?" His face crinkled in disappointment. "If I die, your highness, bury me under the river so I'll be near you forever."

His sarcasm wounded her heart.

Zack yelled obscenities at them for stalling.

Straightening the skateboard, Adam sailed across the alley in his opponent's direction.

Quinn's stomach churned as she watched him. How could he plunge into this joust angry at her? She hadn't *meant* to insult him. Some truths just didn't translate between the worlds.

He and Zack *were* an unbalanced match. In Mandria, such was a sure invitation to death.

Zack sailed into the crowd on Adam's side of the alley, scattering spectators.

He swooped close to the princess, making her flinch. She was the one he was after.

He tipped his skateboard to stop it.

Grabbing Quinn around the waist, he pulled her roughly to him, drawing everyone's attention. The strong smell of spirits gagged her as his mouth covered hers with a sloppy kiss.

Quinn wrenched free, wiping her mouth as her eyes searched for Adam. She caught the pained expression on his face as he turned away.

Zack threw back his head, howling like a crazed wolf.

Then he sailed across the alley, shouting for the match to begin.

19

Reading the Fire

Deep in Mandria, in one of the Marnies' work-rooms, Cam put the finishing touches on a new magic ring.

He'd shaped the ring from gold scraps given to him by Grissel, an old wizened Marnie who'd taught him how to form objects out of precious metals.

Cam glanced up to see if Grissel was still charting his progress.

He was.

The fur circling the Marnie's head was as full as a lion's mane. When he nodded his approval, the fur shimmered golden red in the firelight.

Picking up the ring with a pair of tongs, Cam thrust it one last time into a fire pit. The heat would soften the metal, allowing him to correct a slight imperfection in the curve of the band.

He was careful not to leave his creation in the fire too long, otherwise the markings he engraved earlier would melt.

Grissel shifted impatiently.

Cam knew how hard it was for the old one to watch him work without snatching the ring away and finishing it himself.

Dropping the band into a bowl of cold water to cool, Cam waited while steam rose into the air.

He no longer wondered what had happened to his first ring. Melikar told him it had traveled to the other world with the princess — and he was highly displeased with her for using the magic.

Cam shivered at the thought. Didn't she know better? Even he, with his limited ability, knew the dangers of dabbling naively in magic. They'd both listened to Melikar's lectures too many times for her *not* to know it.

According to the wizard, Quinn wasn't being selective with the magic. Granted, she'd been exposed to enchantments many times in Mandria, but she'd never held such power in her own hands.

Cam remembered the first time Melikar allowed him to cast a spell. The sense of power was overwhelming. He imagined how much greater that power would seem to an unenchanted person.

His mind flashed to his dream of Quinn's pursuer.

He hoped she _would_ resort to magic if she found herself in danger.

Grissel poked him in the side, yanking his thoughts to the present.

Cam reached into the cold water to recover the ring, shaking it dry as he slipped the ornament onto his finger.

He studied it with pride. This ring was better than the other. He'd taken more time to create it.

Was it possible to cast a spell to make its magic stronger? He'd try.

"Perfect." He grinned at Grissel, giving the Marnie a pat on top of his bald spot.

Grissel slapped his hand away, acting annoyed with Cam for distracting him from his own work, yet Cam knew the Marnie welcomed his projects.

Shooing two sleeping kittens off his work table, Grissel returned to his chore of shaping goblets out of molten metal.

Hurrying from the Marnies' cramped chambers, Cam was eager to be away from the heat of the fire pits, and back to the wide, airy avenues of upper Mandria. He rubbed his throat, irritated now from wood smoke.

As he followed the dim tunnels, he wished he could use the ring to whisk himself to Melikar's chamber, avoiding the lengthy hike home.

But until he cast the spell to make the ring *magic*, it was nothing more than an ordinary piece of jewelry.

When Cam arrived at Melikar's chamber, Ameka was there.

She came frequently now, since extra time filled her days — time usually spent tutoring the princess.

Melikar sat in his oak rocker, staring at the fire on his hearth.

Ameka's amber gown ballooned around her as she knelt beside the wizard and began to plead with him.

Cam stopped at the portal to listen.

No one was allowed to disturb Melikar when he was *reading the fire*. Didn't Ameka know this?

Before Cam could warn her, Melikar spoke.

"It is useless to plead with me to send you to the other world."

"But, sire," Ameka argued, "If the princess doesn't know *how* to return, you must teach me the spell, then send me to her so I can bring her safely home."

The enchanter remained silent, gazing into the crackling flames.

"Melikar." Ameka's voice rose in apprehension. "She's been gone almost a quarter moon's turn."

"I know how long she's been gone."

Cam knew his master was concerned about the spell he'd cast on the king and queen. They sat in their living chamber, as silent and still as statues, the pot of tea long grown cold.

Doleran seeds worked for only a limited time. Continuing their use was dangerous. Too much doleran in the blood could be fatal.

Ameka glanced at Cam, acknowledging his presence. "What harm could possibly come from my traveling to the other side of the pool?"

Melikar's gaze shifted from the fire to Ameka. "It could cause insurmountable harm. Already one Mandrian maiden is lost in the other world because of me."

His eyes moved to take in Cam, whose remorse over the whole situation had not diminished one bit. "Why would I allow another Mandrian to travel unprotected to the other side — engaging in spells and charms far beyond her knowledge and ability?"

Ameka bowed her head, yielding to the elder's decision. It was a Mandrian truth.

Melikar dismissed her with a turn of his head.

She rose, nodding at Cam as she passed.

The only sound in the chamber was the popping of the fire and the creak of Melikar's rocker.

Then, in a quiet voice as if nothing had occurred to upset him, the wizard said, "Cam, Ameka, come join me and I will tell you of Princess Quinn's sojourn in the other world."

The two exchanged excited glances. Both were at the bursting point with curiosity over what was happening to their princess.

Eagerly, they sat at Melikar's feet, waiting while he continued his somber reading. After a great length of time, with Cam nearly ready to remind him they were still there, the eminent enchanter began to speak.

"Quinn is well taken care of. She is staying with a family, and has gone to lessons wearing borrowed garments. She has quickly adapted to life in the other world." He sighed. "Too quickly, I'm afraid."

"Is she happy?" Ameka stared wide-eyed into the fire, as if trying to see what the wizard saw.

"I'm afraid not," replied Melikar. "Her visit has been full of strife."

"Over what?" Worry shadowed Ameka's face.

"Conflicts abound. With the young maiden whose home she shares, and with the grandfather, both over different lads."

"*Two* outer-earth lads?" Ameka clapped her hands, looking pleased.

Cam shifted in discomfort. He hadn't thought about Quinn meeting lads in the other world.

Of course they'd notice her; she's beautiful.

Needles of jealousy pricked his heart.

Squinting into the fire, he wished his magic was

as powerful as Melikar's. Sometimes he could see faint pictures in the flames, but did not know how to interpret them.

Rising to his knees, he tried to shake off the uneasy sensations troubling him. "Is the princess in danger?"

"She's in great danger," Melikar answered. "And so is the whole existence of our kingdom." His voice wavered. "Quinn is using the magic unwisely. She shouldn't be using it at all."

Cam studied the enchanter's drawn face, wondering if he should tell of the dream that haunted his sleep.

The wizard turned his eyes upon his apprentice. "It would be better for us all if your ring had stayed in Mandria instead of traveling to the other world with the princess."

Cam sensed a great shudder trembling through Melikar as he continued. "Lad, you must use your power of suggestion to instruct Quinn how to come home. You must meditate as often as you can upon this. Do you understand?"

Cam nodded. "But, sire, _your_ power is much greater than mine."

Melikar didn't react. "Quinn seems to resist every hint I send, as though she knows it's coming from me. When she visits my chamber, she does the same

thing — ignores that which she doesn't want to hear.
You seem better able to reach her than I."

The wizard placed a hand on Cam's shoulder. "Try,
lad."

"Yes, Master." Maybe Cam didn't _have_ to mention
his dream to Melikar. Maybe the wizard was having
the same nightmare.

Yet, perhaps the dream came only to him, as his
hints to the princess were the only ones to penetrate
her mind.

Either way, telling Melikar the dream now was
pointless. He already knew Quinn was in danger.

Cam bade the two good-night, then retired to his
cot in the corner. Why waste time? The princess
needed his help.

Closing his eyes, he relaxed, focusing on Quinn,
trying to envision her in the strange garments he'd
seen outer-earth maidens wearing at the wishing
pool.

Cam recalled each step in the spell to return to
Mandria.

Over and over and over.

He pretended he was sitting with Quinn, telling
her in person:

_Return to the wishing pool. Stand on the footbridge
directly over the water. Wish with all your heart to return_

to Mandria. Turn in a circle to spark the whirlpool. Once it forms, allow yourself to be drawn into it. Do not resist the pull of the magic.

Yet every time Cam listed the steps, his concentration slipped.

First, because his irritated throat had worsened, and the pain kept seeping into his consciousness.

And second, he couldn't ignore the knowledge that Quinn had suitors in the other world.

Cam took a deep breath, renewing his efforts to focus on the princess and the spell.

In the morning, he would ask Melikar to mix a healing potion of slippery elm and white oak bark, with a pinch of myrrh in honey to soothe his throat.

And, in the morning, he would worry about the outer-earth lads who had taken a romantic interest in *his* princess.

20

Twentieth-Century Joust

Quinn held her breath while the jousters squared off, facing each other. Crowds on both sides of the alley backed away, giving them room.

The lads resembled Tristans from the Valley Kingdom, Quinn thought, the way they were dressed in outlandish costumes.

And their lances. Roger had invented a more streamlined version out of broomsticks and foam padding.

Zack wore the oversized shoulders and padded knees she'd seen him wearing earlier.

Adam wore what looked like part of a cage over his face. Padding hung over each shoulder, like a knight's breastplate. On his head was a cap similar to the one he always wore, only made of metal.

The crowd hushed.

In position, Adam and Zack stood motionless, lances held high.

Roger, the moderator, explained the challenge to the crowd: "The jouster who knocks his opponent off the skateboard two out of three times is the winner."

Quinn held her breath while Roger gave a shrill whistle.

Instantly, the crowd came to life as the two lads charged each other.

Adam's hours of practice showed. He knew precisely how fast to push off on his skateboard, at what angle to hold his lance, and when to give it a powerful thrust.

It worked.

The blow caused Zack to lose his balance on the first pass.

He fell hard.

Adam's side of the alley cheered while Zack's side booed.

Quinn slowly released her breath. She'd been wrong about Adam. He knew what he was doing. Skill *could* win over strength.

She relaxed as the lads sailed past each other a few times. For show, she thought, exactly like knights in Mandria.

The cheering crowd and exciting competition made

her feel as though she were at a *real* joust. Granted, no horses pranced by, splendid in colorful trappings. And ladies weren't dressed in gowns, nor knights, mail — at least not the Mandrian type of mail.

And, there was one other difference.

Zack was angry. Furious. In an actual joust, a knight did not show emotion, whether winning or losing. Any kind of reaction would disgrace him. It was a Mandrian truth.

The back of Quinn's neck warmed as Zack hurled insults at Adam.

Adam did not respond to his opponent's abuse. Quinn was proud of him for keeping his honor.

As Zack became more verbal, so did the crowd. Passes on the skateboards became faster and more reckless.

Zack was on guard now, fending off blows from Adam's lance. He hadn't tried to strike yet.

For what was he waiting? A gnawing feeling of uneasiness crept over the princess. She didn't trust Zack any more than she trusted a band of renegade Tristans. They'd look you straight in the eye while robbing your gold.

As the lads made another pass, Zack knocked Adam's lance off-target, as before, but this time, he leaned into Adam, bumping him off the skateboard with his oversized shoulders.

Adam sprawled on the ground. His skateboard sailed into the crowd.

Zack zigzagged a little, but recovered. His supporters roared their approval.

Adam awkwardly pulled himself to his feet, constricted by the heavy garb. He watched Roger, waiting for him to intervene, to disqualify the hit as unfair. No lance was used.

Quinn cringed. Roger didn't tell the crowd any rules other than how a jouster claimed victory. As they locked gazes, Adam's frown told her he shared her thoughts. Of course Zack wouldn't let rules stand in his way of winning.

The princess turned from the lad's disgusting display of triumph — circling his lance above his head, shouting of his own greatness.

The crowd began to chant, "Zack, Zack, Zack, Zack."

Well, if he can bend the rules, so can I. Quinn twisted the magic ring. All the mean things she was empowered to wish upon Zack gave a devilish tickle to her imagination. *What shall I do to him?*

She imagined the shock of the crowd if Zack suddenly turned into a frightened mouse, skittering off down the alley to hide. Quinn chuckled, surprised at how good the idea of being wicked to Zack made her feel.

Adam circled in front of her, completing another

pass. As their eyes met, she had difficulty reading his emotions. His final words echoed in her mind. *I don't need magic to help me win; I'd rather depend on skill.*

She could *not* use the ring. Adam would never forgive her. The humiliation of being saved by a maiden would be too much to bear.

Quinn faded into the crowd, not wanting to witness the rest of the joust. Anything could happen now. The score was tied.

Tension in the air was so thick, she couldn't breathe.

Others moved in front, blocking her view as she backed to the brick wall of the school.

Please let Adam win, she implored the highest spirit.

The thought of Zack's victory turned her heart to ice.

How could she go to the ball with him?

Sarah already hated her because of Zack, and now Adam would hate her because of him, too. Why had this evil lad come into her life and spoiled her journey to outer earth?

The crowd became still and silent as the jousters *whooshed* past each other, again and again, building anticipation.

Quinn couldn't bear to watch, yet *not* watching was torture. Stepping upon a low windowsill, she balanced on her toes until she could see.

Her heart fluttered, watching Adam. His skill was impressive.

The rhythmic roll of wheels on the hard surface of the alley mesmerized the crowd.

Zack gave up on verbal abuse. He needed all his concentration for the last point.

Adam *swooshed* to the far end of the alley, and made a wide turn to start back. A moment before the pass, Zack swerved directly into Adam's path, anticipating a head-on crash.

Adam flinched, jerking his skateboard to the right while Zack turned smoothly away, keeping perfect balance.

Adam tried to recover, but skidded sideways and fell into the crowd.

Zack had cheated again! He was nothing but a despicable knave.

Quinn's emotions broke, bringing tears.

The unfairness of it all made her want to give Zack a few angry jabs — with a real lance.

Quickly she wiped the tears, and burrowed into the crowd, needing to find Adam and console him.

Half the young folk were cheering for the victor, and half protesting the unfair match.

Poor Roger. He'd have to justify the unclear rules. It was her fault, too. She shouldn't have been so quick to simplify Mandrian jousting customs.

Quinn looked everywhere, but her knight had obviously ridden off on his twentieth-century horse. She didn't blame him for leaving to nurse his wounds alone.

"Hey!" Zack hollered, circling her on his skateboard. "Come and kiss the winner." He pulled off his helmet and grinned at her.

Quinn had an unroyal urge to slap his smirking face.

He circled again. "I guess you're all mine for the *ball*, as you call it."

He slid to a stop in front of her, hopping off his board. "What happened to your ride home? The loser afraid to show his face?" He took her arm as he picked up his skateboard. "No problem. Let's go."

"I'm taking her home," came Roger's voice from behind.

Quinn almost hugged him in relief. Yanking her arm from Zack's grasp, she hurried away with Roger.

But not fast enough to miss Zack's departing growl, loud enough to scorch her royal ears: "Tomorrow, little cousin. Tomorrow is the match between *you* and *me*."

21

The Princess's Choice

Morning crept into Adam's room, waking Quinn from her dream about Cam.

The apprentice had been telling her something important, but she couldn't concentrate on his words because her throat felt irritated and sore.

Swallowing, she flinched in pain.

If she were in Mandria, she'd ask Melikar to mix his healing potion of slippery elm, honey — and whatever herbs made the magic work.

Shaking the dream from her mind, she wondered if Adam ever came home last night. She'd waited for him until she could no longer stay awake.

Sarah had come in early from her tryst with Scott, but went directly to her chamber and closed the door.

Quinn sat up, smoothing tangled hair. How was she supposed to get through the day?

And tonight's Halloween ball, her memory added, bringing her fully awake.

Why couldn't everything go back to the way it was before?

Before Zack.

Quinn dressed in her new jeans, remembering how uncomfortable they'd felt the first time she'd worn Sarah's.

Now she liked them and wished they were fashionable under the river. They seemed a sensible thing for Mandrian maidens to wear in the cool, damp air. Running and climbing would be much easier. Granted, she was no longer *supposed* to do such things. . . .

Quinn put on a soft blue garment Adam had chosen. Blue was his favorite color. Maybe if he saw her wearing it today he wouldn't be so angry with her.

Adam.

She hurried into the living chamber. He wasn't there. He wasn't anywhere in the apartment. Maybe he left early with Roger. To avoid her?

Sarah was gone as well. She'd been riding to school with Scott instead of taking the bus.

Mondo was absorbed by what he called the morning news, and didn't have much to say. When she complained about her throat, he offered a tumbler of water and two buttonlike objects to swallow. She wondered if his medicine worked as well as Melikar's potion.

So much for her plan to stay at the apartment. Yesterday, she had to go to school because of the joust. Today, finding Adam was crucial. She needed to amend their misunderstanding, and reassure him of her affection and loyalty.

Mondo was concerned over her ill health. He took her to school so she wouldn't have to face a noisy bus ride.

What met her eyes when she arrived was a shock.

Scholars were dressed in bizarre outfits. One lad sprouted purple hair; another had no hair at all. Unfamiliar eyes gazed through masks of monsters, animals, or distorted humans.

One scholar wore a bedsheet over his head with holes cut out for eyes. Another oozed blood from a knife protruding from his forehead. Quinn hoped it was trickery.

The gaiety in the hallways lifted her spirits, making her realize how long it'd been since anything had caused her to laugh.

She stepped into a girls' room to comb her hair. Only a few days had passed since she and Sarah had shared amusement here in front of the looking glass, yet it seemed much longer.

Two maidens entered. Quinn finished brushing her hair, then pretended to brush it once more so she could listen to their conversation — and stare at their odd clothes: one was dressed as a green-faced hag, ugly as any under the river. The other was a mouse, complete with a long tail, rounded ears, and whiskers.

The maidens were plotting to *cut* homeroom so they could *cram* for a first period exam.

Quinn wasn't sure what *cut* or *cram* meant, yet she could translate the meaning. Not going to homeroom sounded like a wonderful idea; the *last* person she wanted to see today was Mr. Muench. Surely he'd send her to the headmaster's chamber to explain the whereabouts of her records.

Perhaps she could tell the headmaster the information didn't exist because she'd had a private tutor all her life. And if he wished to contact her tutor, all he had to do was wrap a letter around a rock, address it to *Ameka of Mandria*, then heave it into the wishing pool at Wonderland Park — ha!

Since the sole purpose for Quinn's presence today was to find Adam, she gave the maidens a silent *thank you* for the idea to avoid classes.

Feeling daring, yet guilty for breaking rules, she stepped into the hall, hurrying as far from homeroom as she could get. At least spending most of the day in the library would give her plenty of time to record her thoughts and impressions in the journal.

The unexpected holiday kept her entertained during class breaks as she searched for Adam, avoided Mr. Muench, and hid from Zack.

Finally, Quinn persuaded a maiden to lend her a pig mask, which sported long eyelashes and blond hair. She tucked her own endless hair under the back of the mask. With this disguise, the princess passed both adversaries in the hallway, and they never knew it was her.

Was Adam hiding behind a disguise, too? Is that why she couldn't find him? Discouraged at her failed task, she met Mondo after school, thankful for a quiet ride home with few questions asked.

The week's end meant lessons were over for two days, giving her great relief. What should she do about the next quarter-moon's turn?

Staying at the apartment appealed to her. Besides, who needed lessons when the whole world came into the Dovers' living chamber via a box with moving pictures?

Quinn shook her head at the enormity of her plan as Mondo's car headed down the last avenue toward the apartment. Was she actually contemplating *not* returning home?

Was she, the Royal Princess of the kingdom of

Mandria, willing to give up her throne to stay in this world? Nevermore to be a princess?

Princess Nevermore.

Quinn glanced at Mondo, wondering how shocked he'd be if she blurted out her idea.

Her inner voice — which sounded an awful lot like Ameka — argued against her plan: *"You'll never become queen."*

Does it matter? Quinn argued back. *Is that what I truly want? Adam made it sound so boring when I tried to explain it to him.*

Queen Quinnella had always sounded funny to her anyway. *Princess Nevermore* sounded better, yet even that title made her sad.

Arriving at the apartment, she wandered to Adam's chamber to rest and continue her musing. If she *did* abdicate her throne, who would be next in line?

Ah, yes. Dagon, son of her father's sister. She loved Dagon. He was funny and charming. They'd practically grown up as brother and sister, until his family moved to Twickingham, in the outer reaches of Mandria, to oversee his father's gold mines.

Dagon would make a fine king for the people of Mandria. Besides, she'd always suspected he fancied Ameka, and wondered if he'd ever come looking for her. That match would please Quinn.

And her own match? The princess considered her

future as she pulled a quilt around her for warmth. When Adam finished his schooling, they could start a new life together.

In Mandria, she was expected to marry at sixteen.

Well, she would. She'd marry Adam. Then her worries about choosing one of the young noblemen due to come courting would be over.

Would her father approve of Adam Dover? A lad who didn't come from nobility — yet whose family had some vague connection to Mandria?

Pain twinged her heart at the thought of the king choosing a match for her, then being trapped in a loveless marriage.

Such had happened to other princesses before her, according to Ameka, and was certainly a lonely existence.

Quinn could hear her tutor's inner voice again — this time with a warning: "*A hasty decision is thrice regretted.*"

"Oh, you'd love Adam; I know you would," she whispered to Ameka as she hugged Adam's pillow. "In my heart, I've chosen my prince."

And after they married? She and Adam would have heirs — no, children. Plain outer-earth children — not princes and princesses.

Would her parents be proud of their ordinary grandchildren? Surely the king and queen would allow her family to visit Mandria, and would welcome them.

Quinn pulled the quilt tighter, wondering if the life she was choosing *sounded* perfect simply because it *was* of her own choosing. Oh, the thrill making choices gave her!

She sighed.

Now all she had to do to make her fantasy come true was convince Adam to forgive and forget — then hope to the highest spirit that her chosen prince returned the love she felt for him.

22

Mondo's Story

After all her decision making, the princess dozed.

When she awoke, Mondo was gone, Adam still wasn't home, and Sarah had left a note saying she was off with friends to prepare for the evening's ball.

Quinn hoped the family wasn't staying away from their own home on her account.

Hunger led her to the cooking chamber. She fixed a light repast of bread and leftover poultry — the first time in her life she'd prepared her own food. It made her feel very independent.

As Quinn gave the last bite of her feast to Katze, who'd been pestering her, the telephone rang.

She hesitated. Someone had always been here to answer the ringing. She wasn't sure how the contraption worked.

It rang again. Quinn moved to the box on the wall,

lifted the handle, and held it to her ear the way she'd seen others do. "H-hello?"

"Hi."

Quinn jumped — first, because there actually *was* a voice talking back to her, and second, because the voice belonged to Zack.

"Yes?"

"How are you?" he asked in a pleasant tone.

She paused, not trusting his friendly manner. "I'm fine."

"I'll pick you up at seven for the dance."

She waited for him to say something sarcastic, as usual.

"Well, that's all. See you later."

Something clicked in her ear, then buzzed. Quinn placed the handle on its cradle, wondering at the change in Zack.

Adam had told her the lad was decent until he started drinking. Every time she saw him, he smelled of spirits. Why couldn't he be nice all the time?

Quinn heard the front door open. She ran to greet Adam, but it was Mondo, carrying her Mandrian gown in a see-through wrapper.

"Adam said you'd be wearing this to the Halloween dance. I noticed it was wrinkled and soiled, so I had it cleaned and mended for you."

A smile lit his face. "The owner of the laundry said

your gown was made from the finest silk she'd ever seen. I told her it came from cocoons of the rare Mandrian silkworm."

The twinkle in Mondo's eyes told Quinn he'd enjoyed jesting about the dress with the shop's proprietress, even though his explanation was correct.

His mention of the soiled and torn gown drew her thoughts back to the moment Cam materialized in Melikar's chamber, causing her to tumble onto the cobblestone floor. Had it happened only days ago?

Her heart ached with homesickness as well as pleasure that Mondo had taken care of the gown for her. She hugged him, practicing the outer-earth tradition she liked best.

Her actions surprised him. "You'd better get ready," he said, handing her the gown. "I want to see how you look before Adam arrives and whisks you away."

Quinn didn't have the heart to tell him she wasn't going to the ball with his grandson. It would be hard to explain. Yet, after all his cryptic words, it might please him if she *weren't* in Adam's company.

Taking the gown, she hurried to change.

Minutes later, Quinn was transformed from an outer-earth maiden into a Mandrian princess. She looked almost the same as when she arrived in this world, except her skin was no longer pale, her eyelashes curled long and dark, and her hair fell free.

This reflection in the looking glass was the one most familiar to her. Except for the canvas shoes. Pulling them off, she hunted until she found her jeweled Mandrian slippers. Katze had batted them under Sarah's bed.

After putting the cosmetics into the pocket of her gown, and brushing tangles from her hair, Quinn found Mondo waiting in the living chamber.

He greeted her with an approving smile, bowing, as was the custom under the river. "You look beautiful, Quinn, like a real Mandrian princess."

His attention embarrassed her. How did he know what a Mandrian princess looked like? "Can you braid my hair?" she asked.

Dividing her hair into three fat sections, Mondo clumsily patterned the lengths into one long braid, stopping at the back of her knees to secure it with a band from his newspaper.

"Quinn," he began calmly as his fingers looped the band, "I think it's time you returned to Mandria."

The casual comment shivered a chill through her. She twisted to face him. "But I'm not going back."

Before he could argue, she ran from the chamber, not wanting to hear his reasons for the request.

"Quinn!"

The tone of Mondo's voice stopped her. A youth

could not defy an elder. As she trudged back, he motioned for her to sit.

Pulling her braid out of the way, she settled stiffly onto the cushions. Curiosity and reluctance battled inside of her.

"You cannot stay here," Mondo said. "You cannot be Adam's girlfriend, or anything else. You must forget him."

"No!" Quinn rebelled at each word. "You're trying to pretend Adam doesn't care for me. But he does."

Saying it out loud made it true; her heart said so. She gazed at Mondo through tear-blurred eyes. "You cannot keep us apart."

The boldness of her statement shocked her. Speaking back to an elder came dangerously close to breaking a Mandrian truth.

Taking a deep breath, Quinn begged the high spirits to forgive her.

"Sire." She swallowed hard, forcing a steady voice. "Why do you wish to keep me from Adam?"

Sighing, the old man sank to the cushions beside her. "I guess I'll have to tell you the truth."

He met her gaze. "I've never told anyone my secret, but I don't know how else to make you understand. You are Mandrian. You don't belong in this world. You belong under the river."

"I'm here now," she argued, wiping her cheek. "I fit in perfectly; it hasn't been a problem at all."

The lie stopped her. "Well, not *much* of a problem."

She twisted her braid through her fingers. "Adam knows I'm different. He doesn't care." At least she hoped her words were true.

"There's more to it than that, child."

Quinn glanced at him. He was beginning to sound a whole lot like Melikar. Pain shadowed his pool-colored eyes, making her forget her own troubles.

Mondo squeezed her hand with a fatherly tenderness. "I, too, am Mandrian. Born and schooled under the river. I come from a wealthy family of nobility, and I don't belong here any more than you do. It was a mistake for me to come and stay."

Mondo's words did not surprise her. Deep inside, Quinn suspected he was Mandrian. Yet what was so terrible about staying in this world?

He watched her face as he spoke. "When I was a few years past your age, I visited Melikar's chamber to entertain myself, the same way you do. I wanted to help him and learn from him — even become his apprentice.

"My mother and aunt possessed the gift of Sight," he added, "so enchantment was part of my heritage."

Quinn's thoughts flashed to Cam. The apprentice

with no family or history. As long as she'd known him, he'd lived with Melikar. Surely enchantment was part of his heritage, too.

"Just like you," Mondo continued. "I was fascinated with the wishing pool and those who came to make wishes." As he paused, his hands began to tremble.

"One day, a beautiful maiden came to the pool. I was captivated by her. She was as fragile as a wood nymph, with dark, dark eyes and hair the color of coal from the Marnies' mines. It was as long as the tresses of Mandrian maidens, too. She looked so wistful and . . . and lovely."

Quinn tried to be patient while Mondo lost himself in memories, but she was dying to hear the rest of the story. He seemed to have forgotten her presence until she lightly touched his arm.

He shuddered, coming out of his trance. "I'm sorry. It's been so long since I've allowed myself to recall this. After the first time I saw the maiden, she came often to the wishing pool."

Mondo turned away so Quinn couldn't see his face. "I fell hopelessly in love with her. I became obsessed with the very thought of her; with seeing her there above the pool.

"I wanted desperately to meet her. Of course, Melikar wouldn't hear of it, but I pleaded with him. He, alone, possessed the power to arrange a meeting. I promised, if he'd send me to this world, I would bring the maiden back to Mandria and make her my wife.

"After much badgering on my part, Melikar finally gave in — on the condition that I return immediately with the maiden."

Mondo glanced at Quinn, as if to assure himself she was listening. "Of course, I knew the girl would be shocked by my popping out of the river and proposing to her. Yet, I truly hoped she'd return my love.

"Melikar made me pledge that the decision to remain in Mandria rested solely with the maiden. If she chose not to stay, I promised I'd let her go. The wizard had the power to send her back, wiping out her memory of Mandria and me."

Mondo's voice wavered from emotion. "I was ecstatic — convinced that once I showed her the world under the river, she'd fall in love with it, and never want to leave.

"I could hardly wait for the next morning. Melikar planned to send me early, so I'd be waiting when she came to the pool, to keep from frightening her."

He raised his brows in question. "I assume you arrived in this world the same way I did, through the wishing pool."

Quinn nodded.

"Once here," Mondo continued, "all I could do was wait for her."

The old man's face changed.

"Mondo, what is it?"

His hands resumed their trembling. "She never came. I—I was frantic. Melikar's spell allowed me to stay above the river for only a short time. I loved the maiden too much to return without her, and I doubted the wizard would give me a second try."

Quinn took hold of Mondo's hands to steady them.

"In spite of Melikar's warning not to leave the pool, I followed a path through the forest, and found the maiden working at a fairground — which is now the amusement park. That's why she came to the pool so often.

"I suppose it was better that we met there, under normal circumstances. We liked each other instantly, just as I knew we would. Although she wondered at my strange clothes, she believed I was one of many young men who'd come to the fair that day.

"Up close, she was even more beautiful. Her name was beautiful, too. Hannah. I invited her to walk with me, so I could explain who I was and ask her to marry me — and to uphold Melikar's request that we return at once. But instead, she insisted that I travel with her into the city. Her friends were having something she called a *social* and she wanted me to come."

Mondo gave a sad laugh. "Watching you on your first day here brought back all those memories of seeing the city for the first time. What a shock this world is to a Mandrian."

Sorrow tinged his face. "Of course, everything looked different in those days."

He took a deep breath. "I knew I had to tell Hannah at once who I was, the same as I instructed you to tell Adam and Sarah the truth. I found it important to have an ally in this world.

"On the way to the social — at which we never arrived — I told her my story. She didn't believe it, of course, but when I tried to convince her to return to the pool with me, she refused. I—I never considered the possibility of her *not* going back with me.

"I was devastated, Quinn. I couldn't bear to return to Mandria alone and, now that I was finally in Hannah's presence, leaving her was impossible. I was sure I'd enraged Melikar by not keeping my promise, but after the spell wore off, it was too late to return. The wizard might have been able to cast another spell from under the pool, but by that time, I didn't *want* to return.

"Hannah took me to her brother's house. He lived alone, so I stayed with him, and found employment carving wood and making cabinets. Working with wood had been my hobby in Mandria, learned from a Marnie named Jol."

Mondo paused, as if rearranging memories in his mind. "In a few months, Hannah and I married, and moved into our own home. The surname we chose — Dover — was the name of a king to whom my grandfather once pledged his loyalty."

Mondo's voice broke. "I never thought such happiness could be allowed one man. Hannah and I were dearly in love. A year later we had a son."

He buried his head in his hands.

Tears streamed down Quinn's face. "See? You wouldn't have given up Hannah for anything in the world. That's how I feel about Adam, and — "

"No!" Mondo jerked his hands away from his face. "My story is not finished, child, there's more. More that Melikar warned me about."

His voice dropped to a shaky whisper. "But I was too taken with Hannah to listen."

Quinn couldn't breathe, waiting for what was to come.

23

The Mandrian Secret

Dusk fell, leaving the room in shadows, yet neither Quinn nor Mondo moved to turn on a light. Mondo leaned against the cushions, resting his forehead in one hand.

After all he's confessed, Quinn thought, *what more can he possibly say?*

He seemed to be searching for strength to finish his story, so Quinn tried to help. "Mondo, I know Hannah died. Adam and Sarah told me. They said you went away, and their father didn't know where you'd gone."

"I never knew Adam and Sarah's father."

"But you must have. He was your son."

"No, he wasn't. And Hannah was not Adam and Sarah's grandmother."

Quinn was puzzled. "But why did they tell me she was?"

"It's what they've been told."

She tried to sort out what he was saying. "I don't understand."

Mondo tilted his head sideways to look at her. "Adam and Sarah's grandmother was Hannah's great-great granddaughter."

Quinn twisted her braid. She didn't want to appear rude, but it seemed the old man had lost his good sense. "That's impossible."

"I know it's hard to believe. Melikar warned me of the time difference between the worlds, but I was too young and foolish to be concerned with it." He squeezed her hand. "That's why you cannot stay here with Adam."

"I don't — "

"Let me explain. I was twenty when I met Hannah. She was eighteen. The year was 1830. One year in Mandria is three years on outer earth. Although Hannah was younger when we met, she soon grew older than me. She aged while I remained young."

Mondo stopped to remember. "When our son was born, the same thing happened. It sounds incredible, but my son and I were twenty-nine the same year. Yet, by the time I turned thirty, he was already thirty-two. I was, and still am, aging in Mandrian years."

Quinn couldn't believe what she was hearing. "But Sarah and I are the same age."

"When Sarah was born, you were already ten years old. In five Mandrian years, you'll be twenty and Sarah will be thirty. Adam will be even older."

The mention of Adam's name made her realize what Mondo was trying to tell her. Still, even with this knowledge, she could *not* abandon her dream. "But, I thought you were *happy* with Hannah."

Quinn watched a tear roll down his wrinkled cheek. The love Mondo felt for his wife moved her, even though Hannah died many, many years ago.

"Oh, yes, child. I was the happiest man in *both* worlds. Hannah was the love of my life. In my eyes, she never lost her beauty nor her youthfulness."

"How many years were you together?" Quinn's voice was barely a whisper.

"Forty-two in this world. But only fourteen Mandrian years. Not long by the standard I was used to. Hannah lived to be seventy. I was thirty-four when she died."

Quinn's mind refused to comprehend the meaning of his words. "But it's wonderful that you had any time at all together. Why are you denying me the few years of happiness I could share with Adam?"

"You don't understand. When I said *happy*, I meant, I was happy with *Hannah*. I was *miserable* with the kind of life we had to lead. We appeared to be a normal couple for only a few years. Then Hannah began to look older. As our son grew, others assumed he and I were brothers, instead of father and son."

"Did you have other children?"

Mondo was quiet a long time, as if deciding how to answer. "We chose to stop having children, lest they inherit the trait of aging in Mandrian years."

"How did you keep people from discovering your secret?" Quinn worried she might need this information if she found herself in the same predicament.

"We moved frequently. At first, people discriminated against us because they believed Hannah had married a much younger man. It wasn't proper in those days. And poor Hannah. It broke her heart to hear our names mentioned in gossip. Then, a few years later, folks assumed she was my mother — which broke her heart even more.

"Finally, we found it easier to pretend we were mother and son to avoid being set apart as different. Then, rumors began about why I lived at home and never married. Whenever rumors became unbearable, we'd move again. Of course, our son suffered the discrimination, too."

Mondo tugged at his beard, lost in thought. "At that point, Hannah *wanted* to go to Mandria. In fact, she begged me to take her, thinking it would be her fountain of youth, and she'd remain young, like me. Unfortunately, it doesn't work that way. There, she'd still age in outer-earth years.

"Besides, I worried the discrimination might be *worse* under the river, since the caste one is born into rules all else. Even though Hannah was a nobleman's wife, she would still be considered a commoner. She'd never be accepted by ladies of the court. I couldn't put her through the trauma of leaving one world to end her pain, only to find deeper pain in the other."

"What happened then?" Quinn's heart was shattering into pieces. Still, she wanted to know how the story ended.

"Eventually, people believed Hannah was my grandmother. We let them believe what they wanted. The strain was too difficult for our son, who, by then, appeared to be my father. He traveled west during the days of the Gold Rush. I lost touch with him; I think he wanted it that way. I'm not sure he ever forgave me for what I put him and his mother through, merely by staying young."

He glanced at Quinn. "I *did* keep track of my family over the years. Giving them all up would have been too painful. They never knew I was watching, but oftentimes a gift would arrive for a new baby, or money would come when most needed, all from Grandfather Dover — even though it may actually have been great-great grandfather. So, they knew *of* me, yet never knew exactly where I was."

Mondo ran a shaky hand through his hair. "The hardest part of all, Quinn, was watching Hannah die." His voice broke as the tears came.

"When two people age together, one can help the other through each stage of life. But what could I offer my wife as she lay dying? Her body had worn out, yet mine was still healthy. I know how much Hannah loved me, but I swear when I looked into her eyes on our last day together, I saw resentment. I saw a loving person who could no longer forgive me for being what I am. A Mandrian."

As the old man gave in to tears, so did Quinn.

Putting her arms around him, they held each other, weeping freely until no more tears would come.

Mondo pulled a handkerchief from his pocket and blotted Quinn's tears, then his own.

She had no desire to hear any more of his sadness, but when he was able to speak again, she let him finish.

"After I lost her, I spent countless years wandering outer earth, cursing the high spirits for not taking me when they took her."

"Why didn't *you* return to Mandria?"

"I considered it, but _I_ would have been discriminated against. I couldn't simply reappear in the kingdom after all those years and expect to resume my status as a nobleman. When I disappeared, I'm sure everyone believed I'd gone to the world of spirits."

He smiled. "Besides, how does one explain a tanned face and premature wrinkles to a Mandrian? I would have been considered an oddity in my homeland."

Mondo tucked his handkerchief into his pocket. "Another reason I chose not to return was simply because I'd grown accustomed to life here. Once you've experienced the pleasure of a rainstorm, felt the breeze tousle your hair, the sun warm your face, or smelled the wonderful scents of the forest, it's quite a decision to leave it all behind."

His Mandrian eyes twinkled for a second as he added. "Did I mention giving up television and cars and microwave ovens? Returning to Mandria would be like going back in time."

Quinn smiled, but knew he was right. Could one who'd sampled pizza be content again with porridge?

Mondo grew serious once more. "Now I have Adam and Sarah to watch over, which is the best reason of all for staying here."

Quinn nodded. Yet one thing still bewildered her. "If your family never knew where you were," she asked, "how did you know to return for Adam and Sarah?"

"Melikar told me."

Quinn gasped. "Melikar *talks* to you?"

"His powers are strong. I can always tell when my thoughts are not my own. He made me aware of the plight of my — " Mondo squinted at the ceiling as he counted. "My great-great-great-great grandchildren."

Quinn still had difficulty believing it.

"He also told me of you. It was no coincidence that we went to Wonderland Park that day. My purpose was to find you and take care of you while you're here."

"But it all happened so fast. How did you — ?"

"Melikar's spells reach deep into this world. That's why he's enchanter of all enchanters. It's a Mandrian truth."

Mondo glanced at the timepiece on his wrist. "Are you ready to leave for the dance?" His question seemed ridiculously commonplace after the conversation they'd just shared, making the worries of the present tumble back into Quinn's mind.

"I suppose."

He caught her arm as she stood. "This truth I've told you must not leave this room." He lifted two fingers to his cheek, giving her the sign of the Lorik.

"It's our secret," she agreed, returning the sign.

Mondo clicked on the lights.

Quinn took a deep breath and straightened her gown, wondering if her makeup was smudged from wiping away tears.

As she turned to leave, Mondo added in a calm voice. "Now that you know the consequences, I expect you to do the right thing."

She nodded, not replying with her tongue because her heart spoke a different answer.

A few years of happiness with one's true love *had* to be worth more than the pain.

Mondo had not swayed her decision.

She fully intended to remain in Adam's world.

24

Going to the Ball

The unbelievable secret Mondo had entrusted to the princess was suffocating her. She had to get out of the apartment.

Bidding him good-bye, she rushed outside to sit on the front steps. Taking deep breaths of crisp evening air to calm herself, she cringed at the thought of what lay ahead.

The *last* thing she needed tonight was Zack.

Right now her heart ached for another young maiden who'd been in love like she was. Only *that* maiden was born almost two hundred outer-earth years ago.

Quinn's heart also ached because Mondo expected her to say good-bye to Adam.

Resting against a step, she arranged her billowing

yards of skirts. Wearing Mandrian clothes again felt odd. Now *they* seemed uncomfortable.

A screeching sound caught her attention.

Below, a car recklessly careened to a stop.

Zack.

Quinn's urge to dash into the apartment and hide was strong. But in all fairness, she must uphold the wager the three had struck. An outer-earth truth. . . .

She was the reward, and, as her station in life commanded, she would honor the challenge as the lads did, holding her head high until her obligation was fulfilled.

Zack did not come up to fetch her.

Quinn descended the stairs with hesitant feet. As she reached the bottom, he sprang from the car, giving her an approving look-over. "Let me guess," he said, scratching his head. "You're a princess, right?"

Quinn's heart faltered before she remembered that her gown was meant to be a costume.

"Where's your crown?" he teased. "We could make one for you out of tin foil."

Quinn lifted her head proudly and looked him in the eye. "My crown is kept in a crystal case in the throne room of my castle to be worn only on royal occasions." She dared him to believe her truthful answer. "It's carved of pure gold and set with seven precious gems."

"Oh." Zack seemed amused at her wit. "That sure beats tin foil."

As they climbed into the car, she examined his costume — leather pants, a vest with no shirt underneath, a scarf tied around his neck, gloves with the fingers cut out, and boots.

His hair was slicked back on the sides. Dangling from one ear was a trinket like Sarah wore. Quinn wasn't sure what his costume was supposed to signify.

Before they could leave, another car screeched to a stop beside them. Zack spoke briefly to a lad who leaned out a window and handed him a carton of bottles, then sped off.

"My friends," he explained, making the car surge forward. He untopped one of the bottles, releasing the familiar aroma that always surrounded him. He took swigs of the liquid as he drove — a little too fast and reckless for Quinn's comfort.

When they arrived at school, Zack took long strides toward the entrance to the gym. Quinn trotted to keep up with him.

Stepping through double doors, the princess stopped, eyes wide, forgetting all about Zack.

The gym had become enchanted. The dimly lit chamber was filled with colored balls floating against the ceiling. Crinkly paper hung in streamers along the walls.

Loud music struck Quinn's ears, different from any music she'd ever heard. The beat was so overpowering, she felt as if her heart had changed *its* beating to match the music's rhythm.

Zack steered her into a corner. He stood next to her a moment, arms crossed, tapping his foot to the music, then gave her a sidelong glance. "Guess the fun's in winning — not in having. At least not until later."

While she was trying to interpret Zack's words, he added, "Gotta go see some friends. Stay here."

He disappeared through the crowd, leaving the princess alone, like a forgotten trophy.

She didn't *mind* being alone. The sights and music hypnotized her. Even the costumed scholars seemed enchanted as they twirled about the dance floor. Most music in Mandria was soft and slow, with deliberate steps to each ballroom pavane.

She wondered if these dances *had* deliberate steps. Everyone moved a bit wildly. It appeared to be great fun — although not proper behavior for a princess.

Quinn glanced over the crowd, searching for Adam.

Would he come to the ball after what happened at

the joust? Would he bring another maiden? Jealousy tickled her heart.

The music was so inviting, the princess could hardly stand still. She wanted to try the dance. If Adam were here, he'd show her how. The least Zack could do was —

"Hey!"

Roger, in his jousting costume, worked his way toward her. He held hands with a girl who looked beautiful in a fuzzy costume with floppy ears and a fluffy tail. Quinn remembered seeing her picture in Roger's car.

Quinn curtsied, even though, in Mandria, the lad would be required to bow before her. She held out one hand. "Sir Roger, I bid you good evening."

He returned the bow, kissing her hand. "Lady Quinn," he quipped, "this is Wendy. She gave me permission to dance with you."

The maiden slapped him playfully. "Go on. I'll get something to drink."

"I don't think they have carrot juice," Roger teased.

Wendy groaned, then pretended to hop toward the refreshment table.

Watching Roger and Wendy jest with each other made Quinn feel even worse about Adam's absence.

Roger grabbed her hand. "Come on; this is a great song."

Quinn followed, trying to catch up. "Wait," she called, raising her voice above the commotion. "I don't know how to dance."

He stopped beside two whirling monsters with shaggy heads. "You _don't?_"

"No." _Not like this,_ her mind added.

"Where in the world are you from?"

She started to say _"Which_ world?" but shrugged instead.

"Doesn't matter; I'll teach you. All you have to do is feel the beat of the music, then move to it."

Young folk around them stared as Roger demonstrated while she stood still. Embarrassed, Quinn wished she could hide again behind the pig mask.

"Will you teach me the steps?"

"There _are_ no steps." He grabbed her hands and moved with her until she sensed his rhythm and moved on her own. Then he dropped her hands and spun around. "You're dancing, Princess!"

Quinn laughed, imitating the movements of maidens around her. It felt wonderful and free. She loved the loudness and the overflowing crowd of young folk all moving together, yet separately.

With the next song, she relaxed. Mr. Muench

danced by with a maiden from homeroom. He looked a little silly, acting like a youth.

Then she caught sight of Zack, dancing with a maiden dressed in a skimpy animal skin and tall leather boots. Why would Zack make such a fuss over bringing *her* to the ball, then desert her for another?

In a few minutes, the music slowed. Couples stepped close, dancing with their arms around each other.

"Do you know how to slow dance?" Roger asked.

She shook her head.

He placed her left hand on his shoulder and took her right hand in his. "Take small steps now, and follow my lead."

It was awkward at first, until she realized he was showing her which way to step by the way he moved her arm. This was much more similar to ballroom dancing.

Once Quinn got the feel of it, she glanced around and was shocked at how close some of the couples were dancing. It was a sight she'd *never* seen under the river. She tried not to watch, but couldn't resist.

Roger fell silent as they danced. Was he never going to mention Adam unless she broached the topic? Her stomach knotted, waiting for him to say *something*. Finally she asked, "Have you seen Adam tonight?"

He smiled, as if he'd been waiting for the question. "No, I came with Wendy. The last time I talked to him, he hadn't decided whether or not to come."

Roger hesitated. "It's none of my business, Quinn, but Adam's my best friend, and he's *really* upset about losing the joust — especially since Zack cheated."

She nodded, taking the blame upon her heart.

"And, he told me you guys aren't *really* cousins, but wouldn't tell me why you started such a rumor. Anyway, he likes you a *whole* lot."

"Still?"

"Still." He squeezed her hand to make his point. "Zack is responsible for this mix-up, not you. Adam knows that. But he tends to let jealousy get the better of him."

"He's jealous of Zack?"

"Sure. Most guys are. Zack has a habit of stealing girlfriends."

"But Adam has nothing to worry about. I'd rather — "

"I'll take it from here," interrupted a slurred voice. Zack jerked her away from Roger's arms.

Roger started to say something, then stopped. Giving her a sympathetic look, he headed back to Wendy.

Zack gruffly clutched her to him, forcing her arms

around his neck. "A bunch of my friends are driving out to Wonderland Park later. You and I are going, too. We need to have a long talk."

He stared down at her. "I want answers this time, little cousin. You have a hobby of playing magician, and I want to know how you do it."

Zack was almost smothering her against him. "Think what I could do with that kind of power." He said it more to himself than to her.

The song ended. Still, he continued to crush her.

When she pushed away, he let go, making her fall backward into another couple.

The other lad caught the princess to keep her from falling. "Are you all right?" he asked.

"Yes, thank you," she said, straightening.

The lad's dance partner was dressed in feathers, with a beak protruding from her forehead. "I'm going to powder my nose," she said to Quinn. "Want to come?"

Zack offered her his hand as a fast song began.

Eager to get away from him, yet not knowing where one went to powder one's nose, or what one powdered it with, the princess eagerly agreed.

Ignoring Zack's outstretched hand, she quickly followed the bird-maiden off the dance floor.

25

The Breaking of the
Sign

"How'd you get Zack to invite you to the dance?" the feathered maiden asked as they wove their way through the crowd.

"I beg your pardon?" Quinn didn't have any idea what she was talking about.

"I've been working on him for *weeks*, then *you* come along — you're new here, aren't you?" She paused, but didn't give Quinn time to answer. "And he goes and asks *you*. What did you say to make him — ?"

Quinn didn't hear the rest of the question because a brown-dappled horse bumped into them. Off came the horse's head to reveal one of the ball players Quinn had seen on the practice field.

"Mi-chael!" the maiden cried, turning away from Quinn and giving him her attention.

Quinn waited, but the bird-maiden and horse-lad were busy flirting and teasing. She didn't want Zack to come looking for her, so she headed toward the girls' room and slipped inside, thankful for a place to hide.

The princess wasn't alone.

Sarah stood in front of the looking glass, arranging her hair. Her costume was a shredded black gown over a black garment and jeans.

As Sarah positioned a pointed hat on top of her head, Quinn worried over whether to leave, or attempt to make amends.

Before she could do either, Sarah noticed her. "Hey," she said softly. "I need to talk to you."

The friendliness in Sarah's voice was unexpected. Quinn moved closer, leaning against one of the washbasins. "What? Is it Adam?" If *anyone* knew Adam's whereabouts, it would be his sister.

The maiden looked confused. "No, it's *me*. I want to thank you."

"Thank me? For what?"

"Well, this is hard to explain, but — " She held out one hand, displaying a thin silver ring with a green stone in the center. "It's from Scott. It means, um, that he's my boyfriend."

Sarah giggled. "Whoops. You probably don't know

what 'boyfriend' means. Um, it means we're dating only each other."

Quinn returned her smile. "That's wonderful. But what does all this have to do with me?"

Sarah gaped at her as though the point she was trying to make was obvious. "If you hadn't come along and taken away Zack's attention, I never would have given Scott a chance."

The maiden faced the mirror to dot color onto her lips. "I was mad at you at first, but Scott was so understanding and *nice*. Getting to know him made me realize how dumb I've been for letting Zack treat me so terribly.

"So," she added. "It was *you* who brought Scott and me together."

Sarah hugged her. "Thanks. I'm sorry I wasn't there to help you at school the way I promised. Can we be friends again?"

Quinn nodded, truly pleased by Sarah's apology.

"And I'm really glad you and my brother like each other," she added. "I'm sure, after tonight, you two can patch things up."

The princess felt as if a great burden had been lifted from her heart. "I'll always value your friendship — like I would a sister's." She gave Sarah the sign of the Lorik.

Sarah's face turned pale at the sign. She started to return it, then curled her fingers into a fist and lowered her hand. "Oh, Quinn, I've done something horrible."

The enthusiasm in Sarah's eyes dulled to a worried frown. "Stay away from Zack."

Quinn cocked her head in question.

"He knows."

A chill iced through her. "He knows *what?*" She was afraid to hear Sarah's answer. "You mean, he knows of Mandria?"

The door burst open and a noisy group of laughing maidens tripped into the chamber.

Sarah's silence was answer enough. Quinn pulled her into a corner so no one would hear. "You told Zack my secret?" she hissed.

Sarah squirmed, absently rearranging her dress. "I didn't tell him *all* of it. He just kept *bugging* me about you. He knows you're different. I don't know how he suspected it."

Quinn took a deep breath to steady her anger. She'd known Sarah was upset — but not enough to break the Lorik sign. Under the river, a broken sign was unforgivable. It was a Mandrian truth.

"I didn't tell him everything," Sarah said in a trembly voice. "All I told him was — you have a special power. I never mentioned Mandria at all."

The princess recalled Zack's words: *Think what I could do with that kind of power*.

Sarah began to cry.

"It's all right." Quinn gave her a motherly pat, like her nanny, Jalla, used to do. It *wasn't* all right, but what else could she say?

The other maidens stopped talking to stare at them in curiosity.

Quinn dropped her voice to a whisper. "I'm glad you didn't speak to him of Mandria. If he questions my *power*, I'll pretend I don't know what he's talking about."

A horrible thought struck her. "You didn't tell him about the *ring*, did you?"

Sarah wiped her eyes on a hand-drying cloth. "I— I don't know. I can't remember."

Quinn bit her lip to keep from saying more. It wasn't her place to reprimand the maiden. A sign of true royal blood was the ability to pardon one who has harmed you — a truth the princess always found difficult.

"Please forgive me?" Sarah whispered.

This new burden suffocated her even more than Mondo's confession. The walls of the chamber began to close in on her. She needed to get out of there.

"It's forgotten," Quinn lied, trying in vain to smile. "I'm truly happy for you and Scott."

Sarah looked immensely relieved. "We're going out to Wonderland Park later. Want to come?"

The remembrance of Zack's command made her head throb. "I'm already going to the park. Perhaps I'll see you there."

Sarah hugged her one last time. "You look terrific tonight," she said, raising her voice so the other maidens could hear. "Just like a real princess."

Their eyes locked in the looking glass — Sarah's bright with renewed enthusiasm; Quinn's dark with the threat of an ancient fear.

26

A Blue Rose

Panic rose in Quinn's chest as she hurried from the chamber.

Veering the opposite direction from the dancers, she disappeared into a darkened hallway.

Couples, scattered here and there, talked intimately. Some were kissing. Quinn tried not to look, but couldn't help herself. Under the river, a lad stealing a kiss in public was scandalous.

Hurrying past them, Quinn rushed outside. Brisk air made her hug herself to keep from shivering.

She leaned against a brick wall to ponder Sarah's words.

The princess knew she could handle Zack. All she had to do was deny anything he might accuse her of — including possessing a magic ring.

Maybe she should worry *more* over Mondo's story.

Why had he sworn her to secrecy? Revealing this newest Mandrian truth to Adam was crucial, yet she'd pledged Mondo the Lorik sign not to tell.

A door creaked open.

Quinn stiffened. She hoped those intruding on her worries were merely an enamored couple, seeking to be alone.

A single dark form appeared. "Quinn?" came a voice from the shadows.

"Adam?" Emotions tumbled through her at the sound of his voice.

He stepped into a shaft of light from a tall lamp in the schoolyard, gazing at her for a long moment before they fell into each other's arms.

"I'm sorry," she whispered, hugging him tightly, as if it would bond their worlds together.

"*I'm* sorry for acting like a jealous jerk," he whispered into her hair. "I've missed you."

Releasing her, Adam pulled a single flower from his jacket. "It's a blue rose. Blue to match your gown and the mood I've been in without you. I want you to wear it in your hair tonight."

He threaded the flower stem into her braid.

"After this traumatic night is over," he said, "will you consider going out with me — and no one else?"

"You mean, you'll be my boyfriend?" Quinn felt very worldly, knowing what the words meant.

He laughed. "Has someone taken over my tutoring job?"

"Sarah explained it to me."

"Sary? Are you two friends again?"

She nodded.

"I'm glad." He grew serious, gazing at her face in the lamplight. "Princess, I've thought about you constantly. I want you to stay in my world."

Quinn's worries jumbled, like pieces of a puzzle. That's precisely what she'd _hoped_ he might say, yet now that he'd said it, she didn't know how to respond.

"I can't go to lessons anymore," she told him, for lack of a better answer. "The headmaster is suspicious."

"No problem. If you stay, we'll get you a tutor — a _real_ one. And you can live with us as long as you'd like. The college I've applied to is nearby; I can come home on weekends. Maybe I can convince you to join me there."

"College?"

"Oh, geez, you keep me on my toes. Um . . ." He paused, squinting at the dark sky to think. "Going to college is like becoming an apprentice. Here, your friend Cam would attend college to become a wizard — if it were possible. That would be his career."

"Career?"

"Yeah. What you do with your life; what you want to be."

"You mean, you *choose* what you want to be?"

"Well, of course."

Quinn put one hand to her head, feeling sure it was going to burst if she received any more incredible news tonight. She'd never considered what she *wanted* to be; she was a princess. Her life didn't offer choices.

Part of her felt pleased, knowing Adam had made plans which included her — yet he hadn't mentioned marriage. Not marrying in her youth — or being betrothed — was a disgrace for a Mandrian maiden.

Quinn shifted, pulling away, embarrassed at being the one bringing up such a topic; it was not her accepted role. "So when do people in your world marry?"

Adam gave a hearty laugh.

She faced him as he leaned against the wall, wondering at his reaction.

"I forgot — Mandrian princesses are expected to marry at sixteen. Here, that's considered a little young."

"There's nothing *wrong* with our ways." Quinn raised her chin proudly. "I even thought of *you* as a possible choice."

"You have?" His voice softened as he brushed stray

wisps of hair from her forehead. "I've thought of you as a possible choice, too."

She didn't know whether to feel pleased or indignant. "It doesn't *sound* as though you've worked it into your plans for the future."

"Oh, Quinn." In the shadowed light, his deep eyes pierced hers to the spirit. He lifted her chin, drawing her face from the shadows. "I love you. I've loved you ever since you appeared on the bus at Wonderland Park and offered me your hand."

Adam gave her a soft kiss.

At that moment, nothing else in either world mattered, except his lips gently touching hers.

"There's a whole other world on this side of the wishing pool," he told her. "I want to show you what it has to offer. After that, you'll be ready for anything, and the *last* thing you might want is to marry me."

"You mean *not* marrying isn't a disgrace?" Quinn shivered, half from the cold night, and half from Adam's nearness.

"Boy, have *you* got a lot to learn. We've plenty of time for weddings."

He slipped off his jacket, wrapping it around her shoulders.

Quinn was disappointed to see he wasn't wearing his jousting costume. Gratefully shoving cold hands into the jacket pockets, she closed her eyes.

Her head swam with Adam's words, yet the burden of Mondo's secret remained like a hidden weight, tugging at her heart, ruining her happiness.

"I'd love to stay in your world; truly I would. But there's something important you must know." Maybe she could implore Mondo to let Adam in on his secret — that way she would not be breaking the Lorik sign.

Adam pulled her close. "Nothing you could possibly tell me will change my mind about you." He smiled. "So, what is it, Princess? What's this *something important* you must tell me?"

Before she could answer, the gym door flew open.

Coldness penetrated Quinn's heart as Zack burst from the shadows, striding toward them with angry steps.

27

Return to Wonderland

The sight of Zack caused Quinn's heart to topple in on itself.

Withdrawing her arms from Adam's neck, she stepped away, then wondered why she bothered to hide her true feelings from Zack.

"Good evening," the lad said in a courteous voice. "Excuse me for interrupting."

Quinn's eyes focused on his face in the faint light. *He's doing it again*, she thought. *Being nice*. She recalled the phone call, and Adam's comment about Zack's changing personality.

"Since you're *my* date for the evening," he said, "my friends are ready to leave for Wonderland Park, so . . ." He gave Adam a sidelong glance, neither friendly nor malicious. "I'll wait for you inside."

Zack sauntered back toward the school.

Quinn was afraid to meet Adam's eyes. "I have to go now," she told him, confused by Zack's sudden politeness. "Maybe he isn't so bad after all."

Adam scowled at the retreating form.

"Are you jealous again?" she teased.

"You're too good for Zack," Adam said without answering her question. "You deserve the best; you deserve me."

They laughed, holding on to each other without saying more.

"You don't *really* have to go with him," Adam finally whispered.

"Oh, but I do. I can't deny my obligation any more than you could deny the challenge to joust."

"Ah, the honorable princess and her Mandrian truths."

He let go of her. "I'll be waiting for you. Please be careful. And," he added, stroking her cheek the way he did the first day. "Remember, Quinn of Mandria, I love you."

His tenderness made her heart melt like butter in a hot cauldron. "At home, we say, *'My heart embraces you.'* "

"My heart embraces you," he repeated. "I like that."

He raised two fingers to form the sign of the Lorik. "Till later."

"Till later," she agreed, returning the sign.

Quinn stepped briskly through the doors of the school, already longing for the evening's end.

Zack was pacing. "Thought you'd disappeared on me." He watched her face for a reaction, then whipped around and headed down the hallway.

Quinn caught the double meaning of his comment, but made a point not to react. She followed, wondering why he walked ahead, instead of at her side.

When they re-entered the gym, the dim atmosphere, music, and strange assortment of weird creatures startled Quinn as much as they had the first time she'd stepped into the chamber.

Zack strode across the gym without stopping. Quinn hurried to keep up, dodging dancers.

A lad she didn't know blocked her path. He was dressed as a walrus with two sharp tusks hanging almost to the floor. She'd read stories of such creatures in the oceans of outer earth.

The lad didn't speak. He simply handed her one of the colored balls tied with a string, then danced away. Fascinated, she let go of the string so she could grasp the red sphere.

The ball rose from her grasp and floated to the ceiling. "Magic," she whispered, watching the ball bob its way into place beside the others.

As she followed Zack, her eyes met Mr. Muench's.

He gave her his usual frown. She waved, knowing how confused he'd be next week when she didn't come to school at all.

Once outside, Quinn realized she still wore Adam's jacket. Should she ask Zack to wait while she returned it? On second thought, maybe she'd be glad to have its warmth at Wonderland Park. Besides, being surrounded with something of Adam's gave her strength to go through with her unpleasant obligation.

When they got into Zack's car, he immediately reached behind his seat to fetch a bottle.

"Want one?" he asked, twisting off the cap

Quinn shook her head. She hated to see him drinking, now that she knew it made him act like a Marnie who'd inhaled too much vapor from gold ore pilings.

They rode in silence. Quinn watched the sights of the city flash by. Outlines of tall buildings reflected the light of a full moon.

Full moon.

Quinn shuddered. Sometimes in Mandria, strange animals or people appeared, usually in outlying tunnels connecting villages or kingdoms. Melikar attributed it to a phase of the moon over the outside world.

Quinn was never allowed to tarry about the kingdom on those nights. She wondered if a full moon caused odd things to happen in this world, too. . . .

Beyond the moon lay the night sky. And the stars.

How many were there? Quinn couldn't take it all in. She would never tire of gazing at the vastness of this world's heavens.

Someday, when she visited Mandria, she'd tell them of outer-earth magic: light without candles, telephones, television — what a stir *those* would cause in the kingdom.

Suddenly Zack swerved the car to avoid hitting one in the next lane. Quinn held onto the seat with both hands, bracing her feet against the sloped floor.

The sensation of traveling at great speed frightened her. Zack kept weaving between cars. After emptying each bottle, he threw it into the backseat and reached for another.

Finally, he turned onto a dirt road, driving under an arch that read: WELCOME TO WONDERLAND PARK. *How odd,* Quinn thought, *returning to the park wearing my Mandrian gown.*

Zack stopped the car and hopped out. While Quinn waited, he pulled off the leather vest and put on his football tunic with the large numeral on the front.

Inside the park, red, white, and blue lights sparkled in the night. Noisy crowds gathered around the same whirring machines that had scared Quinn so much when she first arrived.

Zack hurried her through the crowd, not stopping

at any of the carnival rides or booths. *He must be late for his meeting,* Quinn thought, following him to a shadowed corner near the edge of the forest.

"Where are your friends?" she asked, not wanting to be alone with him.

"They're not here." He took a brisk swig from another bottle he'd hidden in his jacket.

"But you said — "

"I lied."

Nearby, a park attendant urged people off the footpath so he could close it for the evening.

A biting numbness made Quinn wrap Adam's jacket tightly around herself. "Why did you bring me here?"

"There's something you have that I want."

His leering grin chilled Quinn to her inner spirit.

The lad stepped close. "You know how to make things happen. You have some kind of . . . of power."

"No, I — "

"You can't deny it; I've seen you do it. More than once. I even waited for you to use the power during the joust — but you didn't."

He bent to her eye level. "Why *didn't* you?" His eyes were red and a little out of focus. "You had the power to make Dover win."

Quinn met his gaze. "I don't know what you're talking about."

"Don't lie to me; I know about the ring."

Shock bolted through her. Sarah *had* told him.

The thought of Zack gaining control of the magic ring choked the living breath from her.

He snickered. "Think what I can do with it. No one will mess with me again. I'll zap them and they'll be dead." He raised his bottle high in the air. "I'll have all the money I want. I'll have *anything* I want."

Devil dust, Quinn swore, begging the high spirits to forgive her.

The wood nymph's story sprang to mind. The earth had once been filled with magic. Until evil men stole the power from enchanted creatures for their own wicked greed.

It was happening again.

Zack wanted her magic for his own evil purposes.

"Show it to me," he hissed, grabbing her by the shoulders.

Quinn flinched, vowing to go to her grave before allowing Zack to take the ring.

Use the ring now, her mind warned. *Stop him with the magic.*

No, she argued. *Then he'll know I possess the power. He'll be after me all the time; I'll never be safe from him.*

Her mind reeled, searching for a way out. She could *not* let this happen. *I'll get away from him without the magic.*

Quinn struggled, but he wouldn't let go of her shoulders.

Zack was so much bigger, he could take the ring as easily as Katze had taken scraps of poultry from her earlier.

"Give it to me!" he demanded.

The princess worked at the ring with her thumb until it slipped off her finger and dropped deep into the pocket of Adam's jacket.

Now what?

Suddenly voices broke through the trees as the final hikers emerged from the footpath.

Zack let go of her, acting as if nothing was amiss. He stepped away while the small crowd passed.

Sarah and Scott appeared on the path, hand in hand.

"Quinn!" Sarah cried, waving, "Are you having a good time?" She ignored Zack, who in turn, ignored her.

"Um — " Quinn's mind went blank. What could she say to alert Sarah to the danger? "I — "

"Yeah, we're having a great time." Zack waved the two off. "See ya around."

"Well, 'bye," Sarah called as she passed.

"Wait!" Quinn cried, slipping off the jacket. "Adam must be freezing without this. Give it back to him for me?"

"Sure." Sarah grabbed the jacket, then ran to catch up with Scott.

Quinn let her breath out slowly. Now the ring was safe.

After tonight, she'd never dare wear it again. She'd find a good hiding place in the apartment to make sure the ring remained safe.

Now that Zack would never possess the magic, there was nothing left to fear. All Quinn had to do was fulfill her obligation by returning to the city with him. Then this horrible night would be over, and she could get on with the rest of her life.

"Can we go now?" she insisted.

"You *bet* we're going," he muttered, along with a few curses.

The park attendant locked the gate leading to the footpath.

The instant he was gone from view, Zack's arm circled her waist. In one quick movement, he hoisted her over the gate, then followed, roughly grasping her arm.

"Come on," he snarled. "You and me are going for a midnight hike."

28

Living Cam's
Nightmare

Zack kept a firm grip on Quinn's elbow, forcing
her down the footpath.

Lamps along the way clicked off, leaving only the
full moon to light the path. Even so, Quinn stumbled
from Zack's urgency.

She gasped, trying to catch her breath.

Royal training had ingrained in her that one held
a pleasant disposition and a mild manner at all times.

Yet even the most mild-mannered princess could
bear only so much. Zack had pushed her to the limit;
she'd maintained her good disposition far too long.

The crimes he'd already committed against Mandria's princess would cost him his head on the castle
green — if the king ever got hold of him.

Digging her heels into the ground, Quinn stopped
as stubbornly as a Marnie's donkey. "Where are you

taking me?" she demanded, jerking her arm from his grasp.

"To the wishing pool." He grabbed her arm again. "I know the pool has *something* to do with your power."

Oh, Sarah, why did you tell him of the pool? Quinn feigned exasperation. "I don't *have* any power. Don't you listen?"

"You have a ring; I've seen it." Zack jerked her hands from the shadows into the moonlight.

"It's gone. Where'd you hide it?"

She didn't answer. He took hold of her shoulders and shook her.

"You're hurting me!" she yelled, forgetting to control the anger flooding through her. Tears came into her eyes from the pain he was inflicting, but she blinked them away. Zack was *not* going to see her cry.

"I don't care if I'm hurting you," he growled. "You might as well tell me how to do the magic. I'm not taking you home until you do."

Quinn struggled, but he held on tightly, his fingers digging into her shoulders.

"Holy bats!" she yelped, kicking him in the leg.

Startled, Zack loosened his grip and swore at her.

Twisting away, she ran, gathering her full skirts to keep from tripping.

Moonlight made the path easy to follow, but it also illuminated every hiding place.

Zack's heavy footfalls pounded after her.

Terrified, Quinn wished she'd broken her honorable agreement and gone home with Sarah and Scott when she had the chance. Staying was foolish, yet she never dreamed Zack would harm her.

He'll do anything to get the magic.

Quinn stifled her thoughts — or *were* they her thoughts? Maybe Melikar planted the warning in her mind. . . .

Her heart pulsed as rapidly as her footsteps. Now she was fearful for her very life. A rustling in the trees distracted her as a slight tingle traveled through her.

The trees! They seemed to be reaching out to her. Was the surrounding magic still strong enough to wake the wood nymphs?

Were they trying to help?

Zack was gaining on her. He played sports; he was good at running.

Her Mandrian slippers were not meant for racing, but she kept on, blindly, her chest aching as though she'd swallowed a knight's dagger.

The trees gave way to a moon-washed clearing. The path kept going, so she did, too, frantically searching her surroundings for a place to hide.

Then she saw it.

Ahead, the moonlight danced brightly on the Mandrian River.

Panicked, Quinn rushed straight toward the wishing pool.

All she wanted was to be home and safe — and as far from Zack as she could get.

She wanted to be warm again, wanted to curl up with Scrabit and hide from the heartbreaking truths she'd learned today.

She wanted her mother and father.

She wanted Cam and Ameka.

Even so, a desire stronger than her own safety took hold of her as she ran. She wanted to protect her kingdom and its people.

She, the Royal Princess of Mandria, would give her life to guard the secret of her kingdom's existence.

And Adam? She must protect him, too. Protect him from Hannah's pain, and herself from Mondo's.

"Help me, Cam!" she cried as she ran. "I wish with all my heart to come home!"

As she shouted the words, she touched her finger, feeling for the ring. With a pang of regret, she remembered it was gone.

She was powerless.

Why hadn't she stopped Zack with the magic? And worried later about consequences? She'd always been so quick to use the ring before.

Now it was too late.

Frantic, she could think of only one thing to do.

Reaching the footbridge, she bounded upon it, lifted herself onto the handrail, then paused to glance back, gasping for breath.

Zack raced toward the bridge. "What are you doing?" he shouted. "Stop!"

Quinn took a deep breath and closed her eyes. "Melikar, please, please let me come home."

Gathering her skirts, she jumped off the railing into the wishing pool.

29

Terror on the Footbridge

Quinn's face came out of the water.

Gasping for breath, she shoved hair from her face. Why had she gotten wet this time?

She opened her eyes, eager for a glimpse of Melikar's chamber.

What she saw was Zack, hanging over the railing of the footbridge, mouth gaping as he stared at her.

"What are you trying to do? Kill yourself?" Hustling off the bridge to the bank of the river, he tried to catch hold of her without getting wet.

Arms flailing, Quinn fought to keep her face above the water.

Why am I still here?

Why do coins fall through the enchanted pool, but people do not?

She'd always believed the choice to travel between

worlds was her own. The shock of being wrong choked her with terror.

Without the ring, I can't go home?

The princess sputtered and kicked; legs tangling in her skirts. A strangling sensation consumed her chest.

So. Going home *wasn't* her choice after all. She'd tried twice — once with the ring and now, through the pool.

Maybe she could *never* go back.

The princess gulped a mouthful of murky water. Not going back and not being *able* to go back were two different things.

Mondo's words filtered into her mind: *"After the spell wore off, it was too late to return."*

Have I waited too long?

She needed air, yet her arms grew tired of pushing water from her face. Drowsiness softened the panic.

What went wrong, Cam? My traveling here alone and staying was never part of our plan.

Maybe this was all a dream, and she'd wake in her own sleeping chamber. Her ladies-in-waiting would be lighting candles, and Scrabit ——

Rushing water filled her ears as she was rudely yanked from the river.

Zack carried her over the muddy bank, and up the curve of the footbridge, dropping her without gentleness.

He gave her an angry shake, yelling words that melted away before she could understood them. Kneeling, he covered her lips with his, blowing air into her mouth.

His actions startled and revived her. He was the *last* person in either world she wanted to kiss. Squirming away, she scrambled to her feet, swinging both fists at him.

"I was trying to *help* you." He caught her arms and pinned them to her sides. "Stop acting like this and give me what I want. Hand over the ring and tell me how it works. Then I'll let you go."

Soaked to the skin, Quinn began to shiver. Her gown, full of water, weighed her down.

Disgusted, Zack fumbled with her pockets. "Where've you hidden it?" he rasped, scattering a useless handful of cosmetics across the bridge.

"Don't!" Quinn scurried to recover her possessions, stuffing them back into her pocket. "I told you I don't *have* a magic ring!"

"Magic?" He narrowed his eyes at her. "I never called it a *magic* ring."

Moon shadows gave his grin a contorted wickedness.

Quinn glared at him, distracted by whispers poking at the back of her mind. She tried to ignore them.

Remember, spoke a voice, or was it *her* voice?

Blossoming in her mind was an image of her trip into this world: *Cam. The spell. The swirling water.*

"Quinn!" Zack spat her name through clenched teeth. "If I don't get what I want, somebody's gonna get hurt."

Remember pounded with every beat of her heart.

Her teeth began to chatter. If she didn't get warm soon, she'd freeze to death.

Remember.

The words! The words to the spell.

Cam had been mumbling. No — she couldn't blame him. She *knew* the words; they were burned into her heart. But she was too upset to recall them right now. It wasn't fair.

Remember.

Zack ripped off his jacket, flinging it onto the bridge. "I've had it with your little act of innocence. You're hiding the ring, and I'm going to find it."

The hatred glinting in his eyes horrified her. She shrank back, truly fearing him.

Help me, Cam!

Remember.

Cam!

Zack lunged at her, ripping the front of her gown.

She fought him with all her strength, while the voice inside her head *almost* told her what to do. But not quite.

Quinn pushed away.

Zack flipped her around, hurting her.

Then he yanked her against his chest to make her stop moving.

She stepped around him to keep from tripping over his feet.

Around.

Yes! Around. . . .

She repeated the motion. A soft stirring of water met her ears.

The water in the wishing pool was moving!

Yanking herself free of Zack, the princess twirled by herself.

The lad seized her again.

Clutching Zack's arms, she forced him to spin with her.

"What, the — ?" He shoved her away, as if she'd suddenly gone mad.

Quinn twirled again and again, wet skirts flapping against her legs.

Ignoring Zack, she squeezed her eyes shut to concentrate upon Mandria. Upon home.

I wish it with all my heart.

Magic trembled in her ears, rumbling through her very core, like earthquakes under the river.

Blackness claimed every corner of her mind.

Her last thought was of Adam.

30

The Tapestry Is Unwoven

The blackness surrounding the princess dawned into morning, slowly, the way daylight crept through windows of the apartment.

Her head filled with cottony clouds from the skies of outer earth.

As the mist cleared, she felt strong arms circling her, holding her. "Adam," she mumbled. "You found me."

The clouds melted.

Quinn opened her eyes. She was lying on a cobblestone floor.

Cam knelt beside her, his arms enfolding her.

The princess' heart leaped with an equal mixture of surprise, relief, and happiness.

"Cam!"

Looking as if he'd seen a departed spirit, the apprentice released his hold and leaped to his feet. "I— I beg your royal pardon."

He lowered his head, but Quinn could tell he was grinning.

She struggled to get up.

Cam helped.

The torn, wet gown clung to her slim frame. Hair, pulled loose from the braid, framed her face in damp ringlets.

She threw her arms around the lad's neck. "I'm home!" Her voice was trembly and weak.

Cautiously, he returned the hug, still grinning. "Welcome, Princess," he whispered. "I — we've missed you. You've worried us so."

As Quinn's mind cleared, the realization of events returned in a rush.

Pulling away from Cam, she peered through the wishing pool.

The water still *whooshed* in a circular motion, but slowly. The moon's brightness filtered through the pool, making a pale circle on the floor of Melikar's chamber, shadowed on one side by the footbridge.

A lone figure paced atop the bridge, agitated, stopping every other step to gape into the pool.

Quinn groaned. "Now Zack knows."

"No," came a sharp voice from the shadows. Melikar stepped into the moon circle, mumbling a spell under his breath.

He raised one arm, making a series of quick gestures, then spoke calmly, "The lad with wicked intent will not recall what has taken place. He will have no memory of the ring nor of Mandria's princess."

Quinn squinted through the pool again. Zack stopped pacing. Glancing at his surroundings, he acted disoriented, then snatched up his jacket and disappeared off the footbridge.

The wizard lowered his arm and faced her.

Quinn tried to read the expression on his face — a blend of anger and relief. "Oh, Melikar." She threw herself into his robed arms, startling the old enchanter.

Hugging was not royal protocol, but she didn't care; she'd *never* cared for royal protocol. "I'm sorry I displeased you, sire; forgive me."

Melikar took hold of her shoulders. "The tapestry has been unwoven in the evil lad's mind; the damage, reversed. I will cast another spell upon the maiden and the other lad to erase all remembrance of Mandria and you from their minds."

His words were daggers piercing her heart.

Melikar closed his eyes, mumbling the chant once more.

The thought of living her life obsessed with the memory of Adam, yet knowing *he* would not recall a single hair of her tresses was more than Quinn could bear.

"No!" She thrust her hand to cover the wizard's lips. "Melikar, I beg you in the name of the highest spirit."

The enchanter pushed her hand away, slowly beginning the gesture. "The young maiden has now forgotten."

Tears streaked Quinn's cheeks. "Please don't take the memory of me from Adam. How can you be so cruel?" She pounded her fists against the wizard's chest in a weak attempt to stop him. "I command you!"

Her own words appalled her. She'd *never* used her royal status over Melikar's judgments, always bowing to his authority. Yet it wasn't a true command from the throne — merely empty words spoken in desperation.

Melikar placed a firm hand on Quinn's head, tilting it backward, locking gazes with her.

His translucent eyes shimmered in fiery bursts of red.

The princess held her breath, unable to tear her gaze away from his.

Quivers shuddered through her as though his eyes

burned into her very soul, reading words written in her deepest heart.

Melikar's eyes flashed to normal as he released his grip. Lifting his hand, he resumed the chant. "The young lad — "

Quinn slumped to the floor, sobbing.

" — will always remember."

Quinn raised her tear-smudged face to the old wizard. Without speaking a word, she thanked him from her heart.

He acknowledged her silent gratitude.

A tender smile twitched the edge of his mustache as he helped the princess to her feet. "All others, except Mondo, will forget."

Quinn bowed her head, accepting his decision.

"Cam," Melikar ordered. "Come here."

The apprentice, who had witnessed the scene from the shadows with much curiosity and consternation, sprang forward at the command.

"Prepare the antidote for doleran seeds at once."

Cam rushed to do the enchanter's bidding.

"Princess. Return to your chamber for a dry gown. Your ladies will be bursting with questions. Answer whatever you wish, for the instant you are properly dressed and coifed, they will view you as you've always been, and will not recall your absence. Go about the rest of your evening as though nothing has been amiss."

Pausing, he touched one hand to his forehead and mumbled a chant. "Upon the awakening of the king and queen, the royal attendants will have no remembrance of the lost time or their idle hours."

Suddenly the portal burst open.

Ameka dashed in, pulled by a dragon on a leash. "I was taking Scrabit for a walk, and I — " Her fluttering gaze fell upon the disheveled princess. "Oh, my!"

The two maidens rushed toward each other, then stopped.

Quinn, forgoing royal protocol once more, hugged her surprised tutor as she would have hugged a friend in the other world. Then she gave her pet dragon a good scratching on his scaly neck.

Melikar ignored the gaiety, somberly closing the portal.

The three gathered near to hear his words.

"My children," he began. "The kingdom of Mandria will go on the way it has for countless generations. No one shall mention the disappearance of its princess this quarter-moon's turn. The secret must remain in your hearts."

As if on cue, they shared the sign of the Lorik.

Quinn's heart split in two, contemplating those cherished most dearly. She hadn't known how much Mandria meant to her until it opened its bosom and pulled her home.

Yet part of her remembered another old man she'd grown to love, the sister she'd never had, and one whose image was too painful to call to memory right now.

She'd think of him later. She'd write of him in her journal — ah, but she'd left it behind.

Quinn slipped her hand into the pocket of her gown, making sure *something* from the other world remained. Her fingers curled around the cosmetics, bringing a smile to her face. To compensate for losing all else, she'd proudly walk her kingdom's tunnels with darkened lashes.

Melikar opened his great robed arms, collecting his Mandrian followers. Forming a circle, symbol of eternity, they clasped wrists while Melikar, their wizard, enchanter of all enchanters, proclaimed the newest Mandrian truth:

"The Royal Princess of Mandria has come home."

Epilogue

Adam trudged the path through the forest, head bent, shoulders hunched.

She was gone.

He'd looked for her all night, but couldn't find her anywhere. The princess must have returned to her kingdom.

Yet how could she leave after all they'd told each other?

And how could she leave without saying good-bye?

He thought of their last precious moments together. If he knew he'd never see her again, he would have thought it a fitting good-bye.

Never see her again.

The words ripped his heart. He'd forever be

haunted by not knowing what she had started to tell him when Zack interrupted them.

Adam stepped from the trees into the clearing and headed toward the wishing pool. The water was calm and still, despite a crisp wind stirring leaves in the overhanging branches. Quinn had told him of the spell Melikar cast to keep their window to this world always clear.

Climbing the curve of the footbridge, he sank to his knees, peering into the blue-green pool. *Are you there?* he asked silently. *Will I ever see you again?*

Adam touched the magic ring on his finger, wishing with all his heart for her to appear.

He waited.

Nothing happened.

Touching the ring once more, he wished her his love: *My heart embraces you.*

A gust of wind blew something against his knee. Adam picked up the blue rose he'd woven into Quinn's braid the night before.

Plucking the petals, he dropped them into the wishing pool, one by one.

About This Point Fantasy Author

DIAN CURTIS REGAN is the author of many books for younger readers, such as *Home for the Howl-idays* and the *Ghost Twins* series. She began writing *Princess Nevermore* in 1975 as a short story, but it refused to remain as such and gradually grew into a novel. Ms. Regan is from Colorado and presently lives in Oklahoma.

Experience Worlds You've Never Known

POINT FANTASY

SHADOW OF THE RED MOON
by Walter Dean Myers

A decision has come down that Jon must leave Crystal City — he is forced into the Wilderness where he finds that everything he's been taught is a lie.

Princess Nevermore
by Dian Curtis Regan

Princess Quinn of Mandria ends up on Earth and is alone, confused, and lost. Will she ever get back to her kingdom? Does she even want to?

Now Available in Your Favorite Bookstore

PF397